# *Praise for Edith Bruck and her books*

"*This Darkness Will Never End* subtly draws us into the complex emotional world of growing up in wartime. These are finely wrought, meticulously translated stories about living through both everyday and extraordinary hardship—Bruck, unsparing and insightful, is a major Jewish voice."

—**Jamie Richards**, winner of the National Translation Award in Prose, and translator of *Adua* by Igiaba Scego

"Edith Bruck's spare, haunting, fable-like stories reveal the enduring echoes of history through narratives of survival, loss, and resilience. Bonner's sensitive, masterful translation of this landmark collection preserves the poetic soul of Bruck's prose, ensuring that this vital work will find its rightful place in world literature."

—**Jenny McPhee**, translator of *Family Lexicon* by Natalia Ginzburg, on *This Darkness Will Never End*

"The gifted translator Jeanne Bonner has done a great service by bringing us these extraordinary stories by the Hungarian writer Edith Bruck, a Holocaust survivor who lived in Rome after the war; she offers vivid and poignant stories about the experiences of Jewish families whose lives were overturned during the war. Bruck's book is a splendid and vital addition to the body of Holocaust literature by women."

—**Lynne Sharon Schwartz**, author of *Disturbances in the Field*, on *This Darkness Will Never End*

"Brutal but hopeful . . . Sobering in its considerations and denunciations of ascendant fascist movements."

—***Foreword Reviews*** on *Lost Bread*

"Riveting."

—**Jewish Book Council** on *Lost Bread*

"*Lost Bread* is part of the great autobiographical accounts of the Shoah and the deportation."

—***Agence France-Presse***

"Impassioned, unforgettable testimony of her descent into the underworld."

—**Primo Levi**

"All Edith Bruck's life's work is a testimony, and ultimately the extreme, desperate, word-filled effort to make the incomprehensible comprehensible."

—***Corriere della Sera Sette***

# *This Darkness Will Never End*

EDITH BRUCK

# THIS DARKNESS WILL NEVER END

*Translated by*

Jeanne Bonner

PAUL DRY BOOKS
*Philadelphia 2025*

The translation of this book was supported by a grant
from the National Endowment for the Arts.

This crucial support is gratefully acknowledged here.

Research for this translation was conducted at the
New York Public Library, thanks to a fellowship
the translator received there.

First Paul Dry Books Edition, 2025

Paul Dry Books, Inc.
Philadelphia, Pennsylvania
*www.pauldrybooks.com*

*This Darkness Will Never End*
*Andremo in città*

Published by arrangement with The Italian Literary Agency


Cover photograph (bottom): Edith Bruck's family home in Hungary

Printed in the United States of America

Library of Congress Control Number: 2025931312

ISBN-13: 978-1-58988-201-0

# *Contents*

# *Translator's Introduction*

In the final moments of the title story of this collection, a blind, sickly boy named Beni is on a train with his sister. In an effort to protect him, she has concealed that they are being deported to a Nazi concentration camp. Nonetheless, he expresses bewilderment at their situation.

"This darkness will never end," he says.

He may not be aware of the exact details underpinning that dire moment because he cannot see the gendarmes or the wretched looks on the faces of the other Hungarian Jews seized from their homes, but he can sense the misery around him.

It's a feeling Edith Bruck knows all too well.

The darkness Beni senses is the same darkness that will never end for Edith Bruck. It will never end because she, too, was forced to leave her home—and while she survived, what is contained within the miracle of her survival is the sure knowledge that her parents instead perished, and her way of life was "swallowed up," to cite a phrase from one of her poems, by the death camps.

The quiet domestic scenes of Beni and his sister that we witness in the early part of the story mirror Bruck's pre-war existence growing up in a large family in Hungary. That quiet domesticity is shattered by the war, but Beni's tale isn't only a tragedy—it's also a love story, and the unconditional love between a young girl and her little brother helped inspire a film seen by millions of Americans, even if few of them have heard of Edith Bruck. Film scholar Millicent Marcus and other critics consider Roberto Benigni's 1997 Oscar-winning film, *Life is Beautiful*, to have been inspired by this story, which appeared in Bruck's 1962 short story collection, *Andremo in Città*.



When I began reading Edith Bruck's work, I had already read and revered *If This Is a Man* by Primo Levi, who was her dear friend and a fellow survivor. Levi's work, a seminal account of his deportation and subsequent imprisonment in Auschwitz as a twenty-something chemist, justly informed much of what I understood about the Holocaust.

But I immediately realized Bruck's work was different in one particular way: it foregrounds the voices and experiences of women and children.

This takes nothing away from Levi's towering achievement, as Bruck would be the first to say; she has never gotten over his untimely death in 1987, which she said left her "orphaned" among survivors. Still, her authorial voice reflects pertinent parts of her biography that are infrequently represented elsewhere: she was a twelve-year-old girl when the Hungarian gendarmes knocked on her family's door early one morning in the spring of 1944 and launched them on a treacherous journey that would end at Nazi concentration camps. She was a child when the worst episode of her life unfolded, and the details and nuances of a young girl's inner life abound in these stories.



Given this, it's perhaps not surprising that when Bruck's first book appeared in Italy in 1959, five years after *The Diary of Anne Frank* was published, critics saw her as an analogue for the Dutch girl and viewed her book, *Chi Ti Ama Così* (English translation, *Who Loves You Like This*, published by Paul Dry Books in 2001) as the story Anne would have written had she survived the war. "According to one reviewer, Edith had idealistically picked up the pen where Anne Frank tragically dropped it after being deported and killed in Auschwitz," writes Gabriella Romani, who recounted this episode in an introduction to her translation of Bruck's *Lost Bread* (Paul Dry Books, 2023).

Bruck is among a select group of women writers, such as Polish author Ida Fink, who turned to fiction to illuminate the unspeakable. And Bruck has further set herself apart as a writer who has also probed the murky postwar period when many people struggled to begin again.

Born in 1931 in Tiszabercel, a tiny town near the Hungarian border with Ukraine, Bruck lost her mother, father, and a brother to the camps. Like many survivors, she lived largely as a refugee when the war ended, eventually settling in Italy in 1954. According to scholar Philip Balma, who wrote *Edith Bruck in the Mirror*, the author adopted Italian as a "shield that would allow her to dive back into her painful past without directly reliving the suffering." Bruck has been writing in Italian since the 1950s and she's one of the last remaining great chroniclers of the Holocaust in any language.

This collection of short stories, Bruck's first, presents us with the mindsets of children forced to learn lessons that beggar the imagination, and it gives us insight into the complex nature of survival. Toward the end of the story "Matzoh Bread," the narrator, an adult woman who is visiting Greece after the war, describes meeting a young girl at a dinner: "She was the age I had been when I lost everyone and everything."

It is a searing, succinct summary of the effect of the war on Bruck's every breath. Bruck's deportation and subsequent survival are the seminal events that divide her life in two. Before, she had everyone and everything. After, she had practically nothing.

This collection bridges the two spheres of Bruck's life: before and after. In nearly all of the stories, the Holocaust hovers over the reader—either looming ahead as a fate that cannot be avoided or lurking in the background as the past that can never be escaped. Nothing distracts her from the message she survived to impart, which she expresses concisely in her poem "The Symbol": "Once upon time / there was Auschwitz."

In addition to illuminating a child's view of deportation and survival, Bruck also brings us a female perspective in these stories. The narrator of every story in this collection except one is a young girl. Through these female narrators, we discover the contours of a world where anti-Semitism seethed long before the arrival of the Nazis in Hungary.

The story, "Matzoh Bread," introduces us to a young Jewish girl who loses a friend over a local legend about how the unleavened Passover bread is made. In "Reading French Poetry after the War," a teenage girl struggling to find her place after losing her parents to the war takes solace in French poetry. And in "Come to the Window, It's Christmas," the narrator is a Jewish girl, caught up in her friends' celebrations of Christmas. When her friends arrive below her window as part of a local caroling tradition, they pull a prank that reveals the unspoken tension tearing her parents' lives apart.



Indeed, Bruck, through her body of work, supplies an answer to a question that for me has become crucial: What can women writers tell us about surviving the Holocaust era?

It's a question Levi underlined in an introduction to Bruck's second short story collection (*Due Stanze Vuote*; my English translation not yet published). Calling Bruck's body of work "an impassioned, unforgettable testimony of her descent into the underworld," he drew attention to the way her female narrators grapple with the recurring theme of "lost identity" and the devastating uprooting occasioned by the war. Levi knew women had a unique perspective to share on the Holocaust; he believed they fared even worse in Auschwitz than men, and he attributed this partly to "the haunting presence of the crematoria, located right in the middle of the women's camp, inescapable, undeniable, their ungodly smoke rising from the chimneys to contaminate every day and every night, every moment of respite or illusion, every dream and timorous hope."[1]



Bruck has trained her lens on women in much of her work, translated or not, and perhaps most notably in her nonfiction book on speaking to Italian schoolchildren about the Holocaust. The book's title, *Signora Auschwitz*, comes from her encounters with students who had so little knowledge of the Holocaust that they would confuse her last name with her topic. In it, Bruck describes her survival as an "endless pregnancy" and the enduring memory of the camps alternately as the fetus of "a monster" that she can never abort or deliver, and as "a rampaging tenant inside," metaphors that crystallize the complex and harrowing experience of being a survivor, from a female perspective. These descriptions provide a new way of contemplating the horrors of the Holocaust that is not found in works by Levi or Elie Wiesel, without diminishing what they, too, suffered.

Bruck is considered by some scholars the most prolific writer of Holocaust narrative in Italian. But she

1. From his introduction to Liana Millu's *Il Fumo di Birkenau* in the English translation by Lynne Sharon Schwartz, *Smoke Over Birkenau.*

is first and foremost a storyteller who can create and evoke worlds. What emerges in these stories is a portrait of Hungarian peasantry that pays loving homage to her parents—and a lost way of life. And these fable-like tales don't only tell us about the darkness that will never end but also about the desire to "wake up in a new world," where one "can already see the first lights of the city." In wonderful detail, they flesh out difficult peasant lives brightened by familial love and hope for the future.



Bruck's parents were wretchedly poor people who were rich in worries, in grief, in struggles, and she has vividly fictionalized their peccadilloes and hardships. Little could be more colorful than the scenes that emerge in the story "The Verdict," about a young girl who visits the fearsome shochet—the inspector who slaughters livestock and determines if it is kosher—to learn whether the meat her family planned to eat is *trefa* or if it will pass muster. Bruck's descriptions are often cinematic, which is fitting since she has also worked as a screenwriter. As the narrator turns away with a bloody duck over her shoulder, she threads her way through a dense crowd of both Jewish and Christian neighbor women. Eying the Christian women, the narrator notes,

> I knew they were there to haggle over the rejected fowl that were deemed impure, offering scrawny chickens that couldn't have weighed more than half a kilo. When I walked by, they would say, "I hope it's *trefa*." They knew this word very well, and I would

> look at them angrily, once even saying to a pregnant woman who stroked my duck, "I hope your child is born *trefa*!"

The composite and lightly fictionalized portrait of Bruck's mother that emerges in these stories is one-of-a-kind: deeply devout but also sharp-tongued as she deals with a well-meaning but hapless husband while mired in poverty. In "The Verdict" she chastises her husband, saying, "Your children make you nervous and yet they didn't make you nervous when you were making them . . . only now that it's your job to raise them, take care of them, play with them!" In another story, the narrator tells us, "In our house, everything belonged to Mama and everything was forbidden." The world we are being introduced to is a matriarchy.



Bruck dedicated this collection to her father, and the father figures we encounter here are highly fallible but lovable creatures, desperately maintaining optimism in the face of crushing poverty and anti-Semitism. In the story, "My Father's Horse," the family patriarch tells the truth about his business affairs only when he's talking in his sleep. In another, he agrees to help a neighbor who offers him a dairy cow rich in milk if he can find a husband for the young Jewish girl the neighbor has impregnated (wait till you see how the father solves this conundrum!).

It is a thrill to know American readers will gain entry into this world. It's also slightly confounding; in Italy, Bruck is mentioned in the same breath as Primo Levi.

Her 2021 book, *Lost Bread*, was a finalist for Italy's most prestigious literary award. Pope Francis read the book, including its final chapter entitled "Letter to God," and asked to meet Bruck—at her apartment. When I visited Bruck a few months after their meeting, she breathlessly showed me the menorah he'd brought as a gift when he paid homage to her decades of bearing witness in Italian schools.

That's how important she is.

She is one of a cohort of women writers who have transformed their pain into stirring survival literature, in some cases many decades after the war had ended (unlike Bruck), and in almost all cases in the shadow of male authors whose stories formed (and continue to form) the template for the public's understanding of the Holocaust.

As a literary translator, I have set out to find important Italian women authors whose works have been overlooked by English-language publishers. With the publication of this collection, a clear omission in the canon of classic modern Italian works that have been translated into English is corrected. What's more, it adds to the collective body of work available in English by women survivors who have written about the Holocaust. And what tales they have to tell!

Bruck's story reminds one that new atrocities don't supplant old ones. Edith Bruck does not support what she has called an "endless war" against the Palestinians. In her remarks on January 27, 2025, in honor of the 80th anniversary of the liberation of Auschwitz, she said that every life—every human being—is important and deserving of dignity. Yet nothing that happens today changes the fact that she was seized from her home in the spring of 1944 and taken on a treacherous journey that ultimately left her parentless and without a homeland.

Translating Bruck's words is essential, even if the Anglophone world often pushes such work to the margins. I will never waver in my desire to spotlight and of course translate Bruck's words, because as Levi said, they reflect "the incurable sorrow of someone who . . . doesn't surrender to the void."

This darkness will never end, but, thanks to Bruck's persistence, it has been transformed into literature that will light the way for generations to come.

Jeanne Bonner, 2024

# *This Darkness Will Never End*

*For my father, who got nothing from life*
*And undeserved ridicule from us.*

# *The Frozen River*

From afar, it looked as though there was nothing but forest. The station and the train tracks disappeared among tall rows of poplars, and only a short, sharp whistle breaking the deep silence twice a day without an echo revealed the railroad's presence.

The few people who journeyed to the city arrived at the station two hours before the train departure, and they would sit with their bundles on the wooden benches in the one plain room by the unlit stove. While waiting, they fell asleep, their heads leaning on the shoulders of their neighbors.

From the time I'd finished elementary school, I woke up every morning early and, my heart thumping, I'd run and hide behind the trunk of a poplar. My eyes searched for a boy who had been my desk mate for years and who now went to a high school in the city, along with a few others who were similarly privileged. We'd grown up together, we never argued, and yet now everything had changed. It seemed like he went out of his way to ignore me. I was ashamed to approach him. He'd suddenly grown up, even in my eyes, because they called him "young man," and he wore the blue uniform with the gold stripe and carried a nice leather bag full of new books that he no longer wanted to show me. He said I couldn't understand those books and I wanted to curl up in shame, so I went home with my head down and no desire to eat. This was why I hid from him at the station, and once when he saw me, my full cheeks got even redder, two autumn apples, as he would say to poke fun at me when we were still going to school together.



For a few months, we only encountered each other on the village's main road on Sunday, a day off for him and laundry day for me. Endre and his family went to mass at eleven o'clock while I, barefoot and disheveled, would teeter under the weight of the clothes I had to wash at the river. It would have been better not to cross paths but there was only one route because the church was right next to the river. Nor was it possible to convince Mama to switch laundry day to Monday, when the Christian Sabbath was over. I decided to move up the time for washing so I would be free earlier. Then winter lent me a hand by icing over the river, allowing the rich kids to skate from one bank to the other, beneath the dam. When Endre saw me with two tubs full of clothes, he offered to carry them for me. My raw hands were stuck to the handles of the tubs, my heart beat like that of a hunted rabbit, my cheeks burned like lava and my lips were unable to say anything more than, "Thank you, but I can manage."

Even Endre seemed less arrogant out of uniform; he didn't speak up like he did with his pals at the station, he didn't laugh at me like he did when he ran into me with his parents, nor was he cheerful and easygoing like at school. He only restated, "I want to help you, Erika. The buckets are heavy, and you can catch cold standing still. Let's go."

"I don't mean they don't weigh a lot, but it's a small task and I enjoy doing it," I lied, "even if my mother usually prefers that the big, heavy woman who does the doctor's washing do ours, too. Do you know her?"

"I don't recall," said Endre, "but I believe there was a burly washerwoman who died two years ago of pneumonia, if she's the one you mean. I don't know any others and my mother does the washing herself, like you."

"There are other washerwomen," I insisted. "You're a boy, and you don't know about such things."

"I think everybody should wash their own dirty laundry," Endre replied.

"Of course," I said, and I sped up my stride to keep pace with my heart. Endre followed and tried to take one of the tubs from my hands, but I wouldn't let him because the two helped me balance on the icy road and kept me from fainting.

"You're such a dope," he said. "You won't look at me and think only of hiding when you see me. What did I ever do to you?"

"To me? Oh nothing. You're just conceited and always running around with your school friends. You say I don't understand anything and I'm a dope and that I can't look at your books."

"I don't remember now but if the books interest you that much, I can show them to you," Endre said.



We'd arrived at the river and from the bottom of the bucket I fished out the hatchet and made a hole in the ice. Then without a word, I began rinsing the smallest pieces of clothing so Endre wouldn't see me struggling with the big sheets, which weighed more than a net full of fish when I pulled them from the water. My hands burned in the icy water while my feet froze in my rubber boots.

Endre stood there silently watching me for a while. I liked the silence, as cold as the river and the woods, broken only by the swishing of the clothes and the rushing of the water under the layer of ice.

"A year ago, you were always happy—you talked and laughed so much that the teacher forbade you to laugh even when everyone else did," Endre said.

"I was a child then," I replied.

"What, now you're grown up?" Endre said, smiling. "Even if you're done with school, that doesn't mean you're grown up."

A snowball hit the back of his ear and I turned around. Bela and Jani, two of Endre's school friends, poked their heads out from behind a bush, winking and laughing like fools. I knew them well and had never liked them; now, in their bright school uniforms, which they didn't take off even on Sundays, I really disliked them.

They kept laughing for no reason and mimicking Endre, whom they considered their leader. Bela was carrying two pairs of skates, which glittered in the sun, still new, and began putting on his pair, after pulling the skate key out of his pocket. Endre put on the second pair, then leaning on each other for support, they took a few steps in the snow on tiptoe and were off. They glided across the ice, and whirled around like acrobats; I watched in secret, not wanting them to enjoy my amazement or prevail upon me to compliment them. Jani stayed back with me and he talked endlessly about their school and the city where he had to relocate with his whole family. I wasn't listening; something inside kept me from doing so. What I really wanted to do was argue with him and I smothered my rage by wringing out the sheets and slamming the clothes into the tubs. My eyes roamed up and down the river where Endre, elegant and at ease, glided along. He would wave to me every now and again, gesturing for me to come skate with him, but I gathered my things and hurried toward home.

His voice caught up with me, on the road.

"Are you really angry with me? Erika, wait! Why didn't you say goodbye? Wait! I promise to send some pretty postcards from the city and a photo of my school."

"Oh, I had a wonderful set of them that my father brought me," I said. "One day when we didn't have any paper at home, my mother used my postcards to light the fire!"

"I'll send you two every week, maybe even three," said Endre, "and now give me a tub or I'll be forced to think you're angry with me."

"What will people say if they see you with the bucket?" I asked Endre who now seemed kinder. "You study, you don't do chores. If your mother saw you, she'd be angry with me."



"She allows anything that makes me happy," Endre said. "Your hands are frozen. Take my gloves—they're lined with fur."

"I don't wear gloves," I said. "My father has bought many for me but if I put them on, I lose them."

We walked past his house and after a short distance, we arrived at mine.

"They haven't lit the oil lamps at home," Endre said. "Papa is incredibly frugal. To save oil, he doesn't even let me study at night. That's why I've decided not to come home during the week anymore. I'm going to rent a room with Jani and Bela near school. It even has electric lights."

"You didn't say you weren't coming back anymore," I said in a tiny voice.

"I'll be back every Saturday and leave again Sunday night," Endre replied. "And I'll send postcards that you're going to like. We can see each other on Sundays—you can come with us to the river, if you want. Wait for me at three o'clock under the big tree, the one near the path going to the river."

"What about the washing?" I thought out loud. "I have to do the washing every Sunday."

"Do it on Saturday."

"That's our Sabbath," I said curtly. "It's like Sunday for you."

"Well, then, Monday or Tuesday. It's all the same, no?"

"That's what I think," I said, "but not my mother. She doesn't understand a thing."

"See you later," Endre said. "You'll get the postcards and then three o'clock Sunday by the tree you know."

The next morning, I didn't go to the station. I spent half the day waiting for the postman, even though I knew it was too soon to get news from the city. Pali, the postman, approached me riding his rickety bike whose parts—held together with twine—made a noise like sheet metal struck by wind. Braking with his foot on the front tire, he narrowly missed running into me.

"I don't have anything for you," he said with a teasing smile.

"What's it to you?" I shouted.

"If I bring bad news, you all get angry with me," Pali replied. "If I don't bring any news, it's even worse, no?"

Pali was always cheerful, his light eyes laughing beneath locks of wild blond hair; he looked like the nomads they say originate in India. On the rare occasions that he had a letter for us, my mother would give him a piece of cake if we had some, or bread with butter and garlic. His pants were patched, like his bicycle, but I never saw a happier face than when he would plunge his bony hands into the black leather bag and, moistening his finger, flip through the mail to read out the names.

The next day, I received my first postcard. It read, "Wait for me on Sunday. Endre." The day after: two. The first read, "I'll be back Sunday. Bye." The second read, "This arrow shows the window of my class. Next year, I'll move to the second floor. Do you like this postcard?"



My mother began to worry.

"I asked him to send them to me, Mama."

"Well, who's paying for the stamps?"

"They only cost a few fillér, Mama, and when I have many, many postcards, I'll return them to him for his collection. What's wrong with that?"

"Well, it's up to the two of you but I wouldn't like it if his mother got angry with me. She's very possessive of her son."

Pali looked at me knowingly. In the days that followed, he learned to hand the postcards to me unseen. I didn't worry about anything, I thought about my important appointment and how to take care of the washing that day. So at dawn on Thursday, without telling my mother, I splashed water and washing soda on the dirty clothes, then lit a fire under a large pot for the washing. As soon as my mother opened her eyes, she said, "Who's in charge here? Who gets to decide and give the orders?"

When I said nothing, she pressed me. "What have you got into your head to do on Sunday? I hope you don't want to go to mass or out with your friends. You want two Sabbaths a week?"

"I want to go skating with Endre," I said. "He's promised to teach me and he's only here on Sunday."

"We do the washing Sundays."

"It would be so nice to have the same day off and be with friends."

"Your whole life is a holiday!"

My mother was watching me and I tried to wash everything right, as she'd taught me.

"Now it's the end of the world if you don't do the washing on Thursday. Maybe on Saturdays now you won't eat meat? And Mondays you won't have noodles? On Tuesdays, will you not eat beans?"

"If we ate noodles on Thursdays and beans on Monday, what difference would it make?"

"Order," my mother said. "Habit." All the while, she watched my every move, checking on how I was doing the washing.

Finally, she said, "Don't wring it inside out. It looks like you do a better job with the washing on Thursdays."

I seized my chance, and asked excitedly, "So am I allowed to go skating on Sunday?"

"You want my permission, too?" Mama replied. "Everyone has his own holiday to celebrate and his own cross to bear. Do you really want two of each? Stop pestering me and be thankful that I won't mention it to your father. He mustn't know where you're going or with who, you understand?"

I hugged my mother so forcefully that I slipped on the soap and we both ended up on the floor, getting soaked and laughing like two good friends.



That evening, my mother sent me to Endre's house to borrow two eggs. Our families were so close that my siblings and I called Endre's mother "Aunt." Lately, though, every time I went over to ask for something, my heart would race. So I was glad to find their large kitchen enveloped in the dark of evening where they would not be able to read the emotion on my face. I was glad I didn't have to look Aunt Ethel in the eye. They were all sitting by the fire, Endre's two brothers, his father, and his mother, who was making dinner.

After saying our hellos, Aunt Ethel said to her oldest son, "Go see how many eggs we have." Then she wiped down a bench with her apron and offered me a place to sit. She complained as usual, asking me to excuse the mess and ruing the fact that she'd only given birth to sons who were even messier than pigs.

"None of them brings me satisfaction anymore. I don't even have the joy of having my son Endre at my side, but I'm willing to make any sacrifice for him. You understand, don't you, Erika? You went to school with him—you know how smart he is. I can't put him with the cows and the horses, with the talent he has. He's too delicate to work in the fields. He was born premature and I suffered a lot for him. But one day, he'll be a doctor."

"Doctor, my foot!" the father grumbled. "All I

know is supporting Endre's costing me more than all of the stables and the dog, and I have to pay two other hands to work the land that one day will be his!"

"Do you know he'll be back Sunday?" Aunt Ethel said, unfazed. "I'm packing something good to eat in his suitcase because the poor boy eats so little in the city. Those priests will wind up ruining his stomach and he'll get sick again."

"Poor boy," came the other brother's retort to his mother. "We sold two cows to pay for his wardrobe!"

"You're jealous," Aunt Ethel said. "Endre can't live in the city the way we live here in the country. And you're being unfair because you want for nothing in this house."

Aunt Ethel was kind when she was talking about her son Endre, but out in the street on Sundays, she liked to put on airs while going to mass. Behind closed doors, she opened her heart to me and my mother, yet outside she didn't allow herself to be seen as a friend of Jews. She feared the others would think she wasn't a good Christian, and she denied socializing with us. And besides, my father annoyed her; she never understood what he did in the evenings, holed up at home and bent over a candle reading immense tomes yellow with age.

"Whatever does he do for work?" Aunt Ethel often asked.

"My father is a teacher," I would say.

"A bit of an odd one, going from town to town all week teaching your language, which sounds like Esperanto to me," she said. "If he bought a plot of land, your mother wouldn't have to send you here every other minute to ask for something. I don't mind giving it to you"—she added—"that's not why I'm saying this. It's because it would help out your family a whole lot. Although a Jew wouldn't even know how to plant a nail in the wall."

The old man said to his wife, "Make me something to eat." Then he pointed to me with his cane, which never left his side, saying, "You'll be a gossip, too. All you women do is talk!"



I took the eggs from Endre's older brother and, mumbling a word of thanks, I sped away toward home so I could tell my mother everything.

"Fine people, just a little untrusting toward us," Mama said.

"We keep to ourselves in this house, too," I said. "Not even once have you and Papa invited them over to eat."

"It's not done," my mother replied. "Good friendships matter but not so far as sitting down at the same table together."

I sighed. "It would be so nice."

"You're my little yearlings. If I didn't keep you close, where would you end up? When I haven't any more strength, I'll let you go wherever you want. Be proud of your father. He's a scholar. And let them talk. Aunt Ethel's mind seems covered in cobwebs, for all she uses it."

From a distance I saw Endre check his wristwatch twice and his impatience made me happy.

Coming out to meet me, Endre said, "Have you finished the washing or was the washerwoman resuscitated?"

"I did it on Thursday because I don't want the whole town giving me a nasty look on their way to mass," I said. "You think I'm wrong?"

"Don't worry about other people. No one in the city pays attention to their neighbors."

"The city is different, isn't it?" I asked Endre, who took hold of my hands so he could put his gloves on them. Then he put his arm around my waist and held onto me through the snow, steering me into the woods where he'd already set up a clean plank of wood between two tree trunks, and we sat down. It got dark very early, the shouts of the skaters down on the river came to us muffled. I felt happy and carefree, and when he unfastened my hair with a sudden movement, I let him.

As if guessing how I felt, he said, "I'm happy when I'm with you."

I hesitated before replying. "You must have other girlfriends now, women with red lips," I said finally.

Stunned, he said, "Who are you talking about? Have you gone mad?"

"It's easy for you. You're in the city all week, and you send those postcards . . . Do you think that's enough? I work and work, I do the wash, and they don't even buy me skates."

Endre burst out laughing. "I don't feel like skating today or even seeing my friends. I came for you. I brought you my books. Here."

We began leafing through books of history, geography, and literature together. I caught sight of a poem by Endre Ady.

"I like him because he has your name," I said. "Listen to this."

I had trouble reading it, it was a hard poem and it was already so dark I struggled to decipher the words. I was chilled to the bone, my voice trembled. Endre closed the book for me and put it aside. I could feel one of his hands touching my hair and his fingertips as he opened and closed a barrette that was still latched onto a lock of my braid.



"Don't cut your hair," he said. "It's so beautiful, and in the winter, it keeps you warm."

"Aren't you afraid of the dark?" I asked. "I wouldn't have the guts to cross the woods by myself!"

"But with me?"

"With you, yes."

He went on, "And without me?"

"If I knew you were on the other side, waiting for me . . ."

"You make me feel mature," Endre said. "But I'm only a year older than you. Do you remember how odd your nose was? We would make fun of you, and now you have much bigger eyes than before and a smaller nose."

For the first time since we'd known each other, Endre hugged me and kissed me on the cheek. I wouldn't have been able to do anything to defend myself from his embrace had I wanted to, because I felt myself suffocating, and as though I'd gone silent forever. We took leave of each other that afternoon without anything more. Endre promised to whistle again under my window to wish me good night.

"Having to wait a week so we can see each other for three hours is one more terrible injustice in the world," I thought to myself. An invisible wall of habits and biases divided our families.

I could still feel the warmth of his lips on my cheek and I rubbed it before going inside, for fear the others would suspect Endre had kissed me. Suddenly the postman emerged from the darkness.

"You scared me," I said. "What are you doing here?"

"I was watching you," Pali replied. "I've never seen you with your hair down."

"My barrette fell out," I said. "But it's not the first time you've seen me. Why are you looking at me like that?"

"You're nearly a woman," Pali said, and he hurried off.

At home, my father was sitting in his usual spot by the big lamp and it seemed as though he hadn't noticed my arrival because he didn't even take his eyes off the prayer book. My mother looked me over carefully. My brothers and sisters were curious about where I'd been after dark.

"With my friends," I said, and I began removing clothing.

"You're freezing," Mama said. "Have some tea. We've already eaten."

"So early?" I said. "I didn't have any work to do at home so I stayed out late. I'll wash the dirty dishes right away."

"Tea cups are all there is," my mother said. "But you could iron this pair of pants."

My father got up from the table we used for ironing, and without pausing his reading, he began pacing the length of the room.



"It's lucky he barely speaks so he doesn't question me and watch me the way Mama does," I thought to myself.

I put the small block of coal in the iron and waved my hand over it to rekindle the embers. Everyone else went to bed and I finished ironing the other clothes to warm up from the cold I'd absorbed in the woods. Then, like a cat, I slid into the big bed next to Mama. I struggled to fall asleep.

In the dark, I heard my mother's voice: "What are you thinking about?"

"Skates," I said in a whisper.

"You're sure you're only thinking about skates?"

"Yes. . . .Yes, Mama."

During the week, Endre wrote more postcards, as well as a letter that Pali delivered to me privately because Mama was on the lookout. I did a lot of housework and I was on my best behavior to avoid complaints. Pali had become my accomplice; he sent the letters I wrote to Endre and stamped them since I didn't have a cent. He sometimes played cruel tricks by hiding the letters for a few days. I began to hate him, even though

I knew I needed him. On Sundays when I went to meet Endre, he would follow me like a shadow. Often, I would see him sitting by the hedges along the street, holding a sharp knife that he used to whittle pieces of wood. If I went over to him, he immediately mutilated them into tiny shards that fell like white flakes on the dirty snow. He avoided talking to me until one day I provoked him.

"The figures you carve are beautiful but why make them if you're only going to destroy them?"

"They're awful," he said bitterly. But he regretted it a moment later and invited me to sit next to him.

"You've changed. You used to be so happy when I saw you! I used to envy you. I wanted to be like you and I wanted everyone to be like you."

"Are you serious?" he asked, with a broad smile that I knew well.

"Without a doubt," I said. "But now sometimes you scare me."

"If you want, I can be your friend again," he said sadly. Then he added, "Don't worry, I won't tell anyone you're in love with Endre."

"It's not true!" I shouted. "You're a coward. Endre is just a boy, a schoolmate. But you, you're grown up. You'll be a soldier before long!"

"I understand," he said. "Someone can be in love at your age. But at my age, too, don't you think?"

"I've never said anything about these things to Endre!" I was shaken that someone could read what was inside of me, and shocked at the strange idea that Pali could be in love with a young girl like me. I realized other small matters that I hadn't paid much attention to before: Mama hadn't spoken with Endre's mother much lately, and she rarely sent me to their house to borrow something.

That Sunday, Endre didn't come because his mother traveled to the city to visit him. I tried to find out something from his friends.



"Maybe you miss him?" Jani asked me, laughing.

"No, not a bit, but I wanted to skate with him now that he's taught me how."

"You can skate with us," Bela said.

"You skate well," Jani said. "Why don't you come with us next Sunday? There aren't any girls around here who are good at skating. The ice will melt if you wait for him to come back."

During the week, I ran into Pali again and he said, "He's coming back on Sunday." As he said goodbye, he told me, "Everything will turn out—you'll see." Then he sped away on his bike like someone possessed.

We were sitting in our usual spot between the two trees in the forest. Endre looked a bit paler than usual and he couldn't understand why I was crying. He had just told me that after arguing with his mother he didn't want to come home for a while.

"I'm the real reason," I sobbed. "I know it. Don't tell me, I know. Your mother doesn't want us to see each other anymore!"

Endre tried to console me. "Please don't cry, Erika. I will write you all the time and we'll stay friends even though my mother doesn't want us to."

He kept his hands in his pockets because he'd lent me his gloves once more and he didn't dare look at me.

"I have to study," he said again. "I can't give up my Sundays, I have a lot of hard subjects . . ."

"You're talking like your mother!" I interrupted him with a shout. "I know, I know that you prefer the city, that you'd rather go to the movies with your friends. This is terrible! I can't bear it."

All at once, Endre stood up and he pointed right in my face, saying, "You make me feel guilty—you, my brothers, my father! And now my mother, too!"

He was trembling and he looked extremely pale; I'd never seen him that way. I stopped crying immediately and I swore to Endre I wouldn't start up again.

I felt empty inside, as if suddenly relieved of a burden. We sat together longer than the other times, embracing with our backs against the tree and our legs touching as we looked at the branches bent with the weight of the snow. . . . As it melted, the branches suddenly shot up toward the bold, beautiful sky, freed of their load. The air was mild; spring was approaching.

"Did you cry over me?" Endre asked suddenly.

"I cried over everything that isn't possible for me, and you're among the many things I'd like to have for myself," I said.

"But have me how?" he asked, worried.

"I can't describe it," I said. "I long for you like someone who's hungry longs for bread. Do you know that poem?"

"What silly things are you saying?" Endre replied. "Besides, poetry isn't about bread but about the light missing in a village like ours."

"Bread is more important," I said. "Which would you choose, bread or light?"

"Bread—you're right," Endre said. "This verse you came up with is very beautiful."

"I'll write more for you. We have plenty of time to write to each other, don't you think?"

Returning home, we took the long way, going from the dam to the barracks. It was nighttime, but the windows projected squares of light onto the street, already cleared of snow. Holding hands, we jumped from light to dark, dark to light, until we were under the last window of the army post. Endre dug into his pocket and pulled out his wallet.

"Take this photo of me," he said.

I looked at it for a long time before replying. "You haven't changed at all," I said. "You have a straight nose, a high forehead and a lean face like at school, but your hair is darker now. You were once almost blonde, remember? And your eyes: look at them, round like an owl's . . ."

Endre was laughing as I looked from the photo to his face and back again.

A policeman appeared and shouted, "What are you two doing? You don't have any light in your house?"

"Not electric light," I said, laughing.

"Oh, you want that as well, do you?" the policeman said, as Endre pulled me by the sleeve, murmuring that we should leave right away.

"See how well we can see with the electric light? It's like it's daytime. It must be so beautiful in the city."

That night we talked about everything and nothing for so long that I couldn't bear to go in the house. I coughed a few times before pushing open the door.

"Come inside," Mama said, "I know you're out there."

My brothers and sisters were sleeping. My father was sitting in the kitchen, his elbows resting on a large book, which was open, but he wasn't reading. He took a moment to look at me, and it felt like eternity. Then he said, "While I teach the language of Israel to hundreds of children, my own children ignore the Scriptures and allow the root I planted under this roof to die!"

I listened to my father with great fear.

My father slowly got to his feet. "Erika, do you know where Israel is?"

He seemed like a menacing giant intent on crushing me.

"The washing will be done on Sunday," my mother said.

"Silence!" my father roared. "I asked you a question, Erika."

"Israel," I stammered. "Israel is beyond the deep, dark forest, and if we manage to overcome obstacles and cross it, what awaits us is joy, light, the sun . . ."

I was so frightened that I began to cry.

"Good girl," my father said. "The most important thing is what you feel inside. You picture our land exactly right."

But my mother wasn't as convinced. She turned to my father and said, "The washing will be done Sunday, right, Yankel?"

"The washing will be done on Sunday," he said after a brief pause. Then he went back to the table and immersed himself in reading once more.

Shaken, I got under the covers. Mama had to use chamomile and then kind words to calm me down.



"Papa scares me," I murmured.

"Never mind that—he's a great man," Mama said. "Now go to sleep."

Some weeks passed, and the first sunny days arrived. The ice melted and the river, now free, began to move, meandering lazily. I would see Endre's friends as they went to mass every Sunday morning while I made my way to the river with buckets. I tried to approach them, but their mothers shot me withering glances. All the women were dressed in black and the handkerchiefs they wore on their heads revealed only the center of their faces, which seemed to bear an air of reproach toward me.

I rinsed the clothes, and the water now flowed quickly toward the Danube and the city where Endre was. I sat down under our tree and I wasn't aware how much time had passed until suddenly it was dark. I didn't dare move, thinking I'd only have the courage to walk through the woods if I were certain of seeing him on the other end. I felt a hand brush against me and I shuddered for a second. Then I shouted out, "Endre, you came! I knew you'd come."

"It's me," said Pali, the postman. "Don't be afraid. I came to look for you and take you home. If you want to wait for him a little longer, I'll wait, too. But why don't we go home? The river freezes over only in winter and no one will be coming to skate for a very long time."

# *My Father's Horse*

My FATHER OFTEN talked in his sleep at night but it was hard to understand what he was saying. At first, my mother didn't seem to pay much attention to his raving, and we children laughed about it when we weren't sleepy. One Saturday night, my mother woke me so I could listen to what my father was saying, but I demurred, saying, "I'm not getting up in this icebox of a house. . . . And anyway, it's no use. Papa talks so fast, you can't understand anything."

"Come on," my mother insisted. "If it's both of us, we'll understand more."

Mama was nearly in tears. So, I had to get up; her heavy body was trembling all over in the dark, and when I took hold of her soft hands, they were damp with sweat.

"Let's go quietly," I said, "because if he wakes up, he won't be talking anymore. Mama, you stand next to him, otherwise you'll get cold, and the two of us will listen."

He tossed and turned in bed, breathing loudly

with his eyes closed. At times, he opened them in his sleep, and this frightened us at first because we thought he would wake up. Instead, he slept restlessly, calling out words or even entire sentences. On this night, it was about a horse, but not even a whole horse. We heard him say, "Half of the horse was mine. We bought it together. Now he says it's dead, but it's alive—he's sold it!"

"Who?" I asked.

"My good-for-nothing business partner," my father replied. He jerked around in bed, sweating. I told my mother to leave him be but she insisted that she wanted to know everything and if he wasn't going to talk during the day, he had to talk at night.

"We left the tavern," Papa said, "and he was trying to make me have a drink outside—he wanted me to forget that the horse was gone. Then he took me to see a very kind blonde woman and I don't know what happened. I was with her in a small dirty house. I remember the sink was stopped up. . . ."

Mama was quietly crying. "Do you see what kind of a father you have?"

I urged my mother to try to sleep, telling her to say nothing in the morning. "Little by little, we'll learn everything."

"I want to leave him," Mama said. "I won't live with him anymore."

"Don't say such things," I begged her. "Wait a few more days."

That night, the same scene was repeated, but my father only talked after a big meal, which we didn't realize right away since that didn't happen often. After that, my mother went out of her way to give him more to eat. Not at midday, however. A heaping meal every evening.

"Deborah, none of you are eating," my father would say. "Why not?"

"You're thin, Alex. You must eat. Your complexion is bad."



My father began to fatten up while the rest of us slimmed down. Mama had dark circles under her eyes and I knew she wasn't sleeping so she could catch every word. Then afterwards, she couldn't sleep because of what she'd discovered.

Suddenly, my mother changed her tactics; every morning she'd interrogate my father about what he'd let slip the night before. He didn't recall anything and he denied it all.

"What are you talking about, Deborah?" he would ask, irritated. "Are you going through my pockets?"

"I know everything, Alex," Mama said. "Who was that whore? And what happened to the horse?"

"What horse?" he said. "I know nothing about it."

But he sounded doubtful and we knew he told the truth in his sleep.

"Alex, you've ruined everything. Don't ever touch me again. Beginning tomorrow, I'm sleeping with Aniko and you'll sleep with Endre. Out of shame, we cannot divorce. What would people say? I couldn't survive, Alex, it's the end."

My father became very frightened and began sobbing. He told her not to abandon him and we were crying alongside him like idiots. My father then promised again that he wouldn't tell any more lies, he wouldn't touch a drop of alcohol and we'd get back his half of the horse. For heaven's sake, the horse was his, too, and it wasn't in any way his fault if they'd tricked him, making him booze up.

"It's not my fault," he kept shouting, "if I'm a wretch who still believes in people and in the valor of men, or if I start believing all over again! But as of today, I won't believe it anymore. You'll see! I'll change. Give me another chance, Deborah."

Mama lifted up her apron to dry her eyes and we looked imploringly at both of them. All four of us ended up in each other's arms.

"I'll leave tomorrow and I'll take care of everything," Papa said. "Don't worry."

"For the children, I'll forgive you," my mother said. "I hope God will forgive you and have pity on me. That way, my time will come early."

Our father left the next day, making endless promises. Resigned, Mama sighed quietly. We awaited his return more eagerly than we had before; at night we would wake up over the smallest noise from outside. His absence pained my mother and every day she'd wonder aloud about when our father was coming home. Each time, we'd say he would be back soon, bringing plenty of nice things. But he was gone even longer than usual. We kept a count of the days and the hours, often going all the way to the train station. My mother pictured disease, death, serious accidents, and she kept praying under her breath, "Please God, send him home to me only this time. I love him just the way he is."

We had nothing to eat and the shops wouldn't give us anything on credit, with the excuse that he'd never be back. After three weeks he returned, and I told Mama not to make a scene; it was what she'd asked for and what God wanted, so better with him than without him. He brought sweets for everyone, and a pair of shoes for each of us, as well as oranges and red apples.



We were happy. That night, I sang and Papa asked Mama to dance, and she stood up while Endre moved furniture to make room. I sang an old waltz tune that Mama often mentioned and I was amazed they knew how to dance. Smiling, they reminisced about old times and I asked Endre to dance and we spun around as if crazed, singing different melodies and bumping up against the furniture, or the two of them, who went on sweetly dancing the waltz.

We paid some of the debts then, and we could make purchases again. At night, my father began talking once more, but I refused to listen. My mother kept interrogating him each morning and they always quarreled. He kept promising he wouldn't tell any more lies, he wouldn't drink again, he wouldn't be so trusting of people, but every time, it began anew. My mother forgave him, suffering over the truth, which was denied her by day but so readily confessed to at night. He went on about the horse while my mother dried the nighttime saliva that pooled copiously on his shirt.

I often said, "How can you lie next him while he snores and talks in his sleep and then in the daytime you have to drag words out of him?"

"When we were young, he didn't snore," my mother replied. "He slept as sound as a lamb. But when you get older, your shortcomings multiply."

One night when we were all ears to hear the rest of the horse story, I climbed into their bed because I barely managed to catch two out of every ten words he said. While I waited, I grew cold and to warm up, I turned over so quickly that a plank in the bed broke and all three of us ended up on the floor. My father must have gotten a terrible scare because he didn't realize what had happened right away.



"What's going on?" he said. "What happened? Did the cart break?"

"What is it?" I said, pretending nothing had happened and wriggling myself free from the wooden slats and straw. Mama lit the oil lamp and I held the light while Papa tried to fix the bed. But he was so sleepy that he spread the straw all around the kitchen, creating a cloud of dust. We had to open the front door and in came a bracing cold that partly woke up my father.

"We need new straw," my mother said. "Half of this is just dust. Can't you tell, Alex? I can't wait until Passover for fresh straw."

"I will get it for you," my father babbled, "but what if we tried going to sleep? We can talk about it tomorrow."

"But you won't remember anything tomorrow. I can't understand it—you haven't put your bottom on the bed yet and your head is already asleep. And with everything that's on your mind! A bomb landing on the roof wouldn't wake you up."

My father managed somehow to arrange the bed and, turning away, he lay down on the side by the wall. I went back to my bed where I could see Mama sitting on the edge of one of the slats for fear it would topple again. I woke Endre to send him to sleep with Papa, but he didn't want to.



"He sputters like a pot of polenta," he said. "You go. You're the smallest."

Mama didn't want to sacrifice the sleep of the weak, pale little boy; she lay down with her son and I carefully slipped into the big bed.

After that hectic night, my father left early, followed by the alarmed gaze of my mother. "Don't say anything, Deborah," he said. "I'll take care of everything."

An hour later, an acquaintance arrived with his son; they had a supply of fresh straw and carpentry tools. They began repairing the bed. My mother watched them with a certain pride.

"What about my husband?" she said.

"He's gone to deal with the horse." His friend said he would be gone a few days, at most.

Two days later, we heard shouts coming from outside. It was nighttime and I was frightened.

"What could that be?" Mama said.

I listened closer to the voice coming from afar.

"It's Papa!" my little brother and I shouted. And,

each of us grabbing a sheet, we shot out of the house looking like ghosts.

Papa wasn't alone. Or rather, there was an immense shadow that moved and swayed with the wind. The moon was out but it wasn't bright enough to see by. I went inside and came running back with a lit candle that went out immediately. My father, however, was now close enough. He held onto a rope that was attached to the neck of an emaciated horse.

"Bring me a lamp!" Papa was shouting. "Then you'll see what an animal, what a horse this is, and in one piece! They didn't swindle me this time. He's a real work horse. I'll attach him to the cart . . . as soon as he recovers a little. He's worn out, he must be hungry."

There was a storage shed on the side of our house covered with a small roof that the wind had yet to damage. We tied up the horse there, then ran inside and out looking for something to give him to eat, and some straw to put down under his legs, which were so skinny they looked as though they would give out any minute. My father was very proud. He said he'd come on foot from the nearby town because the horse wouldn't move, and he often had to hold him up. He had practically dragged him twenty-five kilometers, and now he and the horse both were hungry. Meanwhile, he stroked the neck of the scrawny animal.

"He doesn't know me yet," my father said, "but he'll love me later."

The horse lay down as soon as he was inside, and there was no moving him, not even to feed him. I went into the kitchen to pull apart the bed so I could gather some straw (from our fresh supply), and I put it under the horse's belly. I wanted to call him by name, but Papa said he didn't have one yet. We had only to choose a name because the horse was ours.

"I'd call him Wind," I said, "because if the wind blows, it will carry him away since he's so thin; but if he holds his own, then he's stronger than the wind. Does everyone agree?"



"All right, we'll call him Wind, but this horse is sick," my mother said. "Alex, can't you see?" The miserable beast was foaming at the mouth. He refused to eat, had a little water and lowered his head between his outstretched hooves. We left him alone.

While Papa had something to eat in the kitchen, we bombarded him with questions about where he had gotten the horse.

"I spoke with my business partner about the half that he owed me," my father said. "And this time, he gave me a whole one. I hope"—he looked at my mother—"you will see this as a good deal. It seems simple to me; do you have something to say?"

"He's a beautiful horse, Papa," we said. "And if he fattens up, we can even ride him."

Mama said he was worthless. "He's sick with the plague or something serious. He smells, too."

We went to bed but no one could sleep because we were all listening to every breath the horse took. At one point, he began to bray and kick hard against the wall of the kitchen at the exact spot where Mama and Papa had their bed.

"He's going to bring down the house," my mother said. "This was all we needed!"

We all got up and went outside. The horse was on his back, beating his head against the wall; it was an awful sight. We heated up water to make him drink, we stroked him with wash cloths.

"My sweet little Wind, what's the matter?" I kept saying, and the horse moaned like a person who was suffering. Papa was pale and stiff, while Mama issued orders of all kinds to help the horse who kept hitting his head. We moved him away from the wall with great effort; his legs were wracked with constant tremors and every now and again he shook all over, his breathing labored, and quickening fast. He began bleeding at the mouth. We ran out to wake a neighbor to ask for help; he had horses and knew how to care for them. He brought a large glass syringe filled with a solution, which he injected in the horse's behind and began massaging his belly. Mama was quietly sobbing, and I told her you can't cry over an animal, the Jewish religion forbids it. But Mama wailed harder and said again and again, "Forgive me, Lord!" The straw was completely bloody. After a long bout of pain, the horse died at dawn.

Wind's death filled us with sorrow; we all seemed to be in mourning.

"You see the bad luck that dogs me. Wherever I put my hand, grass won't grow. But is it my fault? They made me think he was still viable. Deborah, do you really think he was sick?"

"Are you blind?" my mother shrieked. "Couldn't you see he was sick? Or were you drunk when they fobbed him off on you? Tell me, you were drinking beforehand, weren't you?"

I said we could forget all about having a whole, healthy horse, since we'd never even hoped to have one at all, but my mother was beside herself.



"Now even the fresh straw is gone," she said, "and we'll have to sleep on bare wood."

My father hastened to say he would immediately replace the straw. As far as the horse went, they would never be able to trick him again with a sick animal. And he added, "I promise you, Deborah, I'll be more careful. It can't always be this way. Things will be different. . . ."

"Alex! I've been trying to believe you for fifteen years, and you swear and cry. You're not a man!"

"And I, Deborah," my father replied, "have been trying to believe in people for thirty years because I have faith in people and in the greater good, and I still do. . . ."

# *Come to the Window, It's Christmas*

My mother made one final effort, and then sank into the big bed. A lovely cloud of white feathers wafted almost up to the ceiling and slowly fell like the snow I could see through the window.

My father turned toward the wall and sneezed twice, causing the flame in the oil lamp to flicker. Then, grumbling loudly, he stuck his head under the covers.

It was one of those high, country beds, all wood and down with pillow cases so worn that feathers flew everywhere at any brisk movement. As kids, we could only climb onto the bed with the help of a stool or with a leap, which always upset our mother: it was her bed, where she'd been sleeping for twenty years, and every feather that emerged was a feather ripped from her heart. That heart was vast, generous, even kinder than the heart of God. No one has ever loved, prayed, mourned, and cried all at once with the same passion as her. She fretted over the old stove, over the broken-down chairs and the wobbly table, the cracked kitchen walls, the few pieces of furniture I bumped into with the broom, even the gas ring on the stove if she caught me darkening my face with lampblack to scare my younger siblings. In our house, everything belonged to Mama and everything was forbidden.

"Raise the lamp a little," our mother said. "It's too dark."

At that moment, the flame went out and there was a dim light from outside.

"Get me the matches," Mama continued. "They're in your father's pocket."

"Where?"

"On the chair. Can't you see?"

I could see just fine but I wanted to keep my parents up, as I waited for my friends to come sing under our window, just like every year, for their Christmas Eve night celebration.

"It's completely white outside," I said, longing to go out.

"How else would December be?" my father mumbled from under the covers.

"It's only eight o'clock, Mama. It's all beautiful and white out there. Everyone else is going out. We're the only ones staying home."

"Have you gone crazy?" Mama said.

"It's Christmas, Mama. I have to go out."

"Do you want to wake up your father? Turn down

the lamp. Cover me gently, like that. Now good night and be quiet."

Biting my tongue, I obeyed her, but I wasn't ready to join my little brother, Edi, at the foot of the bed. I wandered about the house like a cat, and my mother's voice surprised me in the kitchen.

"What are you looking for? The water is in the enamel bucket under the table."

"I'm trying to sleep," my father said.

"Lucky for you that you never have any worries," my mother sighed. "I can't even manage to sleep in the featherbed."

"Why? Are you afraid you'll ruin it?" Papa replied. Then, after hesitating briefly, he added, "There isn't anything to eat, is there?"

I heard my mother turn over in bed.

"Is something wrong, Imre? Before you could sleep even without any dinner."

"Papa, can you imagine how much they'll eat tonight?" I said, happily joining in on the conversation.

"It's a lucky event for the poor and a nice tradition, giving carolers sweets, ham, sausage, and even money!"

Alarmed, my mother said, "You're not going to let her to go out, are you?"

"Oh, I'm not even thinking about that," I said. "I'm saying Christmas is a boon for Christians. If my friends come, you'll give them some change, won't you, Papa?"

"Enough of this talk." My father turned to face the wall to sleep so he could forget his hunger.

"You can't send them away. I beg you, Mama. You tell him, too."

"Don't waste any more breath. Luckily your father's already sleeping."

On tiptoe, I approached the bed. I could hear my father snoring.

"Mama," I whispered, "move his head away from the wall. It's so damp and it smells of mold."

Mama took my father's head in her hands and turned it toward us, laughing in the semi-darkness.

"If you could feel how much it weighs. Who knows what all is inside! It weighs more than the rest of him."

I was laughing, too, as I thought of Papa's slender neck and the way he rested his head on his chest, like an underfed goose.

All in all, my mother was happy to chat because she had insomnia. And I couldn't ask for anything more that night. I was excited, awaiting the carols that would be heard from outside, and couldn't come soon enough.

"I wonder why my brothers never write to me," Mama said.

"It's because of the war," I replied, rushing to say something else so she wouldn't have time to ponder or get worked up to the point of tears, thinking them all dead already.

"Have an apple, Mama," I said to her. "I put one under your pillow. There should be a mandarin, too."

I helped Mama rummage around. We found the apple first, and then the mandarin, which had wound up at the bottom of the bed. It was warm, and the peel smelled like the hair of Roma women. Mama ate the whole thing and I had the apple.

"Your father is the kindest man in the world. He has many faults but I see him the way he was twenty years ago, when he arrived on a sturdy horse and jumped down, knocking the heels of his soft boots so he could ask for my hand in marriage. It was the second time that he was visiting me, and my parents, of course, weren't amenable . . ."

Stopping to listen, Mama didn't finish her thought and extended her bare arm to turn off the lamp. Then she instinctively ducked her head under the covers as if afraid.

"Do you hear footsteps?" she asked anxiously.

"You bet I do!" I replied cheerfully in the dark.

"They're strange sounds," Mama whispered. "You better wake your father. He is, after all, a man."

"Don't be afraid, Mama. It's Christmas Eve."

"You think war observes holidays?"

"They're coming," I said excitedly, and I jumped to my feet on the bed to get closer to the window.

"Don't move," Mama ordered me.

I gazed out the window, holding my breath. Mama had succeeded in spreading her fear. The voices drifting up were muddled. They didn't sound like kids but men speaking an unfamiliar language until a clearer voice shouted, "Everyone out!"

Mama shot up out of bed and ran toward the corner of the room to pack some items piled on the floor into an old suitcase. That suitcase must have been there for a while but I hadn't noticed it. My father also leapt up and feverishly began searching for clothes, his eyes still shut.

Stunned, I asked, "Where are you going?" And I threw open the window.

My friends were below, huddled together in the snow, and they were roaring with laughter. They all had mustaches drawn on in lampblack and they greeted me with a thunderous "Heil Hitler!"

"It's them!" I shouted with joy.

My father appeared at the entrance to the kitchen, his black eyes shining like lit coal. He was crying, perhaps for the first time in his life. My friends noticed it, too.

"We were joking," one of them said. "We didn't mean to scare you."

"Get out of here!" Papa bellowed. "Get out of here, you idiots!"

His voice terrified my friends who fled, forgetting their sausage, ham, and sweets under our window.

My father went out in his stocking feet and was surrounded immediately by a pack of ravenous dogs that squared off as they circled the food. Mama grabbed the broom and ran to help him.

"With you, I can still fight and win," she yelled, swinging the broom.

With a hop from the window, I, too, was in the street to give a hand to my father, ripping the sausage away from the dogs, and gathering the food in the snow.

"That disgusting stuff won't enter this house," my mother yelled.

"Don't shout," my father panted as he kept fighting off the dogs.

"Imre, throw that garbage away," my mother said firmly.

"We could sell it," stammered my father who had managed to save a large clean bit of ham.

"You'll see, Mama. We'll become rich."

"Take it away so I don't see it," Mama shouted behind me as I escaped into the kitchen with the spoils.

As soon as we were all back inside and she'd bolted the door, Mama said, "God has punished them."

"It was a joke, right, Papa? Just a joke."

"Of course, my little one. It was only a joke. Now we can sleep. We'll sell it all tomorrow with the hunger that's going around."

And he smiled at my mother, as if seeking forgiveness for his weakness.

# *"This Darkness Will Never End"*

My little brother Beni pulled me toward him, squeezing my hand with all of his feeble might, and said, "Do you really think I'll get better someday?"

"I'm sure of it," I said, "and now listen to me. Every day at the same time, the train whistles before slowing down. Have you heard it? It doesn't stop completely, but it slows down and we'll have just enough time to jump on. You'll have to be quick. I'll take your hand like now—and then up! Once we're aboard, it's all over. When I spot the big train station, it'll mean we've reached the city. Then we'll get off and look for a doctor. You'll wait a long time, but the doctor's going to cure you."

"Then what?" my brother Beni asked.

"When we come back, we'll walk until we can't walk anymore so you can see everything: the people, the colors, the sky. Even the sun'll shine brighter that day, to celebrate you after so much darkness."

How many times I must have said these words to my little brother, who was seven and I eleven. He may be the one who gave me courage and faith in something better. We dreamed together. Every morning, he asked me the color of the sky. And I would tell him it was bright, a sweet, tender blue, even if it was black as tar. And for a moment, I wound up believing in that beautiful sky, too.

Mama and Papa stayed in the fields all day working while I looked after Beni and our little cottage. I went to school, too, and waited impatiently for summer when I could spend more time with Beni, who suffered all alone for months, waiting each day by the front door until I returned. Merely upon hearing my footsteps, which he could recognize from far away, he would start shouting in delight: "Lenke! Is that you, Lenke? Hurry!"

I often found him crying because he had rotten egg all over the seat of his pants, or a clump of green thorns lodged in his curly hair. To avoid yanking out the hair where the thorns clung, I wound up cutting off whole tufts from his head, leaving bald patches. They were round, soft woodland burrs that the village children gathered to make tiny constructions or balls that they threw at the first person to pass by, ruining his clothes or, worse, his hair.

"Oh, they're so mean!" Beni sobbed. "Look what they did to me today!" And he would show me his pants soiled with tomatoes or rotten eggs.

"My little Beni, it's no big deal," I said. "You didn't notice when you sat down. The same thing could happen to Mama in the kitchen. Just be more careful next time. Touch the seat before you sit down."

"That's not true, you know," Beni said, sobbing. "But you have to help me. You have to help me get even."

"I will," I replied. "I'll set traps outside their house. I'll cut a hole in the ice with a hatchet when they go ice skating. But first, I need to know who's playing these pranks. They'll all fall in the dark, and wind up with a broken leg or an arm in a cast."



Pleased, Beni smiled. He was already picturing the scene and the fearful shouts.

"Would you really do that for me? Aren't you afraid of being found out?"

"If I don't do it, they'll keep pestering you each time I have to bring Mama and Papa their lunch in the fields. Something must be done!"

Happy, we hugged. Beni stayed in the yard while I swept the earthen floor in the kitchen and the bedroom.

"Beni!" I yelled out. "If you hear someone coming, whistle. In the meantime, I'll get dinner ready and chase away the flies."

"Shoo, shoo," I shouted, waving a washcloth at the flies, which often smeared the windows or got in the soup cooking on the stove. I tried to herd them and guide them out the door.

"I want to come inside," Beni said. "It's getting dark. I can feel it."

"We'll eat soon," I said. "It's evening, they'll be home soon."

We sat down in the kitchen and breathed in the aroma of the bean and carrot soup. That day, I'd found some sausage and Beni seemed more content than usual.

"What is our house like?" he said suddenly. "You've never told me the color of the walls or what the furniture is like. And what about Mama and Papa?"

"Our house is nice, with a large woodstove in the kitchen, a table and four chairs, a bed with a thick quilt and green blanket on top. There are also one, two, three shelves for pots. I covered each shelf with colored paper with little figures, like fabric. It's very pretty. It took forever to cut it all out. The flies have already made it dirty—it looks like it has polka dots!"

Beni smiled and asked what the figures looked like. I described them: lots of children, younger than us, holding hands like in ring-around-the-roses. They were all the same, all happy; boy, girl, boy, girl.

"How I wish I could see them," Beni said, lost in thought for a moment.

His thin legs dangled lifelessly from the chair; his sad, pale face looked transparent, the veins visible here and there; his jacket fit snugly around his meager shoulders and made his bones jut out. If I could only give him more life, I thought. He looked like one of those paper figures, so pale and fragile.

"The bedroom is nicer," I said. "Two yellow beds where we sleep, separated by Grandmother's big black wardrobe, the one with the long mirror. And then two marble-topped chests, and on the floor a rug Mama made with scrap cloth. The walls are white and the floor is packed earth but almost smooth. The drapes are really beautiful but they're not up today. Mama only hangs them on holidays so they don't get dirty, along with the large red velvet cover that she promised me when I marry."



Beni jumped off the chair to go outside but bumped into the door. "What's wrong, Beni?" I asked. "Do you want to go someplace? Where?" I grabbed hold of his arm and led him back to his seat.

To reassure him, I said, "I won't get married until you can see me in my wedding gown. I promise."

"I don't want you to marry," he said again, tearfully. "Don't ever leave me."

"I'm never going to leave you, Beni! There are so many things we'll do together. We'll travel the world! Now give me a kiss and let's make up."

"Are you good-looking?"

"You're good-looking yourself," I said. "You're tall like Mama. You're the best looking of all of us. You have delicate skin and brown hair. You look like an aristocrat's son—feel your hands, how long your fingers are. Whereas I have blonde hair and a round face. I'm told that my eyes are a strange color, always searching for something, seeming to cry even without tears. If you really want to know, Papa looks like me and Mama like you. Now be quiet, they're coming, and we won't talk about anything."

As soon as they came in, they sat down at the table. My mother grumbled that I'd put too much oil in the soup, and as usual, I'd wasted everything.

I grabbed the napkins from where we kept the plates and the breakfast dishes to undo the knots.

"Go open those outside!" Mama shrieked. "Can't you see they're full of ants?"

I went out in the dark, and for a moment I thought about not coming back; going somewhere else so I could escape, far, far away.

When I came back into the dim kitchen, I was again gripped by the desire to flee. Mama was making the big bed; Papa was sitting in the chair, his head bowed, already asleep. His hands, smudged with dirt, rested motionless on his stomach; every so often he lifted one to scratch his head or his back. Beni's eyes were open wider than usual, and he stared ahead as if he could see. His eyes were of a shade that doesn't exist; a pink-tinged sky blue, as if muddied with a watery gray. When he stared at me with those eyes, I thought immediately of death, the only real thing present in Beni's eyes.

The scant light came from the candle below the image of St. Stephen on Grandma's chest of drawers. I'd have liked to have the lamp on at dinner, but Mama always said you can find your mouth in the dark all the same without having to waste kerosene. That gloom grabbed me by the throat; it felt like I was suffocating.

"I have to buy a clock," said Mama, who had already climbed into bed.

"A clock!" I shouted with joy. "What color?"

"A nice, white enamel alarm clock, like the one they have over there," said Mama, nodding toward the neighbors' house.

"When?" I asked.

"Next spring, at the market. I have to buy a coat for you, Lenke, you're grown so big and I'm embarrassed to have you going around without something proper. You hear me, Peter?" my mother said, elbowing Papa, who was sleeping. "I want a clock, a coat for Lenke, and a few other little things."



"Yes," my father mumbled in his sleep.

"We'll place it here on the table," my mother went on, pointing to the spot, "and if we have the clock, we'll lay out a bright tablecloth, one that my poor mother gave me as part of my trousseau, and that I'll give to you, Lenke, when you marry."

Beni gave a start, and I squeezed his hand as a signal but he still asked Mama, "When's Lenke going to marry?"

"What's it matter to you?" Mama said. "We'll find her a proper husband, that way your father won't have to work so much."

"Certainly," I said. "But what about the clock?"

"We'll buy it in springtime, if all goes well," Mama said, half-asleep.

I quickly tidied up the kitchen and set out things for the next morning's breakfast, then we went to sleep in the other room.

"With the new coat, we'll go to the city," I murmured to Beni. "And we'll have a clock so we won't miss the train."

The next morning, my mother asked me to bring some warm broth to her in the field because her stomach hurt. Around noon, I wrapped the pot in a cloth and headed to the field where my parents worked.

"Hurry back," Beni called out.

"I'll fly like a bird," I shouted from the road, "and you try not to worry."

When I returned, Beni was at the door, waiting for me. "What a time I've had!" I said. "Come quick, let me tell you."

"What happened?" Beni asked, alarmed.

"I saw two men. Know who they were? The owners of the land where Papa and Mama work. I saw them arrive on horseback and I ran to find out who they were. I've never seen two horses as pretty as they were or such elegant gentlemen!"

"And then what?" asked Beni anxiously.

"Then they get off their horses and ask who I am and what my name is. 'Lenke,' I say. 'My mother and father work here.' 'And you,' the older one asks, 'What do you do?' 'Nothing,' I say. 'I brought them lunch and now I'm going home.' The same man says, 'Who is your mother?' And I say, 'What, don't you know her? She's worked on your land for years.' After looking me over for a while, he says, 'If I had to know everyone who works for me, I'd spend all of my time asking names and repeating them.' Do you know how I talked to that man? The same way I talk to you, simply. Then he says, 'Call for your mother, I'd like to speak with her.' So I shouted, 'Mama! Mama! Come here!' She runs over in a fright, stumbling through the field while also blowing her nose on her petticoat and wiping away the sweat. She bows before the older gentleman and says, 'Yes, your lordship, here I am. Is something wrong? Are you perhaps unhappy with us? Oh, I see the young master is here as well . . .' And then Mama bows again for the son.

"His lordship asks Mama, 'Is this your daughter?' And Mama nods. Then I say to the gentleman, 'So you do know my mother.' Taken aback, he looks at me and says, 'As I told you, I don't.' So I say, 'Oh, you sound as if you're on familiar terms with her.' Alarmed, Mama says, 'What's gotten into you, daughter?' Then, confused, she turns as if to beg the man's pardon. In the meantime, the younger gentleman, who had come closer to get a better look at me, urged his father, 'Ask her! Ask her!' "



Beni interrupted me. "How did he look? Handsome?"

"Not at all. He had a hateful face with a few short teeth like a mouse. And he smelled like a hospital. You know what the man said to Mama? 'I want your daughter. I can use her to replace Viera, our maid who was impregnated by some scoundrel, so I had to send her away.' And Mama says, 'What do you say, Lenke? You would be fortunate to serve the great Televy family.' "

But at that point, in front of Beni, I caught myself before blurting out what Mama said then about the cross she bore, having a blind son to support.

After a painful silence, Beni practically shouted, "But you won't leave me, will you?"

"I wouldn't dream of it!" I said. "Can you picture

your sister serving the household of that pig-faced aristocrat, or saying, 'Yes, young master,' 'No, young master,' to that stupid dead-faced son of his?"

"Are there stupid dead people?" Beni asked, laughing.

"And how! Don't you remember me telling you how idiotic the barber's son looked when he was dead?"

That evening, we went to bed before our parents arrived home. But I could hear my mother shouting all the way from the street. "What a disgrace! It's too much. I can't bear it. I'll show you, if you don't run right over to be a maid. If we die one day, who's going to support you?" With these words, Mama walked into the kitchen, groping through the dark to try to hit me.

"Where are you?" she kept saying. "I know the ground didn't swallow you up!"

The two of us were huddled tightly together in bed.

"I'll split you in half like a log!" Mama was shouting.

"Just try it!" I replied in the dark, trembling with fear. "Lay a hand on us and we'll leave forever."

In the meantime, Papa had lit the lamp, mumbling to himself. I was completely hidden by Beni's body, and my mother's hands hung in the air without reaching us.

"What'll you do without us?" she kept saying. "Lord help us!" The light made her less aggressive. She began to fret. "Nothing ever goes right for us. Why doesn't God rid me of the blind son if he's already taken the other one away? We're alone, just the two of us . . ." And she turned to my father for comfort.

Under the sheets, Beni squeezed my hands, biting his lip to keep from crying. He almost never spoke with them because he felt guilty for being blind. Mama considered him sickly and disabled—she would sob and beg God to give him sight or let him die.



"Come and eat," my father broke in. "Something will turn up. Not all misfortune comes to do us harm. It's best for Lenke to remain home now that she's big, and I don't dare send her to those little princes who salivate just to look at her. Bloody hell!" he shouted, and launched into an unending string of curses until Mama interrupted him, saying we'd already sinned enough to deserve such a fate.

At this, the anger faded, and the dinner ended on an almost cheerful note. We all talked for the first time as grownups and friends, even the two of us. For a moment, it seemed as though our hopes were lighting up Beni's eyes, which stared blankly into space. For the first time, he said in front of all of us, "How I wish I could see you!" Her eyes full of tears, Mama kissed him and embraced him so tightly that Beni let out a moan, and clasping his hands, he ran from the room so no one could see the enormous sobs that shook his weak, little shoulders.

Life went on as before, yet we were united by a stronger bond, which before had seemed at the point of breaking. Beni and I would talk about our revenge for the kids' cruel tricks, which came to fruition in the winter. My traps worked and several people had to go around with their arms in slings or were sick in bed. The village quack was over the moon as he'd never before had a whole winter's worth of business. "God is behind this," he kept saying. "For a long time, no sick people came knocking on my door. I thought I'd lost the people's trust."

I felt relieved after we got our revenge. And doubly pleased to see Beni come back to life and to know that no one got seriously hurt. Oddly, everything worked out for the best. Even the mean pranks stopped, and it didn't take long for the town to figure out the mysterious culprit behind the accidents, although the more ignorant ones still believe it was the work of the devil.



Having resolved Beni's problems, I went back to my favorite pastime, which was following the funeral processions of the rich. I never missed one, and when I returned home, I'd tell my little brother all about it, from start to finish. It was always something special to see, and the most recent one was always, naturally, the best.

"This time," I told Beni, "the dead man didn't look like the girl in the wedding gown. It was an ugly old man this time. But what a gorgeous casket! It was all silver. And there were scores of relatives no one's ever seen, even from the city, with big black hats, embroidered veils and lace handkerchiefs. People were whispering that not even a king could complain about a funeral like that. A plump woman kept pressing the relatives to put gloves and a hat on the dead person. Someone else was crying and asking about the will, and everyone forgot all about the hat and gloves while they argued over the inheritance. Finally, they placed the casket on a cart lined in black velvet and filled on the sides with flowers. The six horses went two by two, outfitted in the same velvet as the wagon, with shiny black bows, each one fastened with a little floral crown."



"It must have been beautiful!" Beni exclaimed. "I imagine circus horses look like that."

"When the procession began," I went on, "people were running out of their homes to see the rich folks in mourning. They made the sign of the cross, their aprons covered with flour and their hands still coated in dough, envious of the dead man's relatives. So I slipped in toward the front and walked with the procession to the cemetery. Then someone took advantage of the confusion in the crowd of onlookers and stole the velvet off the wagon.

"The funeral home immediately demanded that the family pay them for the damages. You should have seen them then! Everyone was saying yes, they were relatives but not so close—just distant cousins—and the immediate family couldn't be disturbed at such a difficult moment. Then in a huff they turned toward the priest who prayed too long over the grave. I went along to the dead man's house where the Roma, dogs, and beggars were already lined up. The meal must have been wonderful. I spied through the windows—it looked like a wedding. Everyone was laughing, drinking and eating. Whole chickens, sweets, roast goose . . ."

"Did they eat a lot?" Beni asked, after a long silence.

"People like that have bottomless stomachs, as Mama says. But come here and try to guess what I brought you." And then I guided Beni's hands, helping him untie the knots in the apron to find the scraps that I'd rescued from the dogs and the Roma, the tastiest morsels or the cleanest pieces.



Summer came, and we'd go out into the fields. We would walk barefoot over the cool grass but Beni would get tired easily. I'd shared my hobby with him and he wouldn't leave me alone about it. He wanted very badly to come along with me to follow a funeral procession up close, and I had to give in once. But we were unlucky. A poor person's funeral isn't any fun; for me, it was always a terribly sad sight. A bony horse would drag the cart with the casket through the town, and the people who came out to look would go right back inside, saying, "It's better this way, the poor thing isn't suffering anymore." Only the village idiot and the little children would follow the few mourners, and then run away laughing. Their corner of the cemetery was bare but so packed with dead people that when they dug the grave for the new casket, old bones turned up. In the summer, there were wooden crosses, but come winter, they would be stolen to burn in the stove.

Between weddings and funerals, a piece of news reached us from afar, brought by the ragpicker who was going around announcing that war had broken out. People gathered in the square. Everyone argued feverishly about the last war and the coming one, and about the nation and the land. Suddenly, my father got called up.

"This is the second time that I'm going to war," my father said. "But this time, I'm no longer young and I believe even less in personal glory and national victory . . ."



We all gathered around him and hurried to prepare his sack of belongings with underwear and wool sweaters. Mama even took out the special holiday linens. We could hear the young men in the street marching toward the station, singing. Mothers were crying, sisters were beaming at their brothers walking proudly in their new uniforms.

"Write home," they shouted.

"Bundle up!"

"Watch out for yourself, son."

My father kept saying, "I won't make it this time. I beg of you all: stick together and pray for me."

In silence, we went with him to the station. My father turned to Beni and, clasping him, said, "Maybe it's better not to see, my son."

Our sobs were lost in the shouts and the tears of the others who were seeing off sons and husbands or who had caught up to them at the last moment with a parcel forgotten in the rush. The train arrived, whistling this time, too, but it stopped for a while. It was full of men in soldiers' dress and the line of train cars stretched into the countryside. Papa seemed to age in an instant; there was hatred in his eyes and he was wringing his hands as always when he was troubled.

He was never one to talk a lot, but now he was quieter than ever.

"Do as your mother tells you!" he shouted from the train as it pulled away. "Help her. And Lenke, don't forget: you're the head of the family now."

The house felt empty after my father left. Mama mumbled night and day, "What are we going to do? What are we going to do? I don't have the strength to struggle anymore."

"I'll work," I told her.

"You're young," she said. "You have your whole life ahead of you, but I don't think I've got long to live. . . . I'd just like to see you get married."

My mother's words struck me; they felt true to me, terribly true, and I wondered what we would do without our parents.

I was almost thirteen years old; I'd thrown away my last toy at six and I hadn't played since. But at least I didn't have the total darkness, in bones and spirit, that Beni had. And I didn't have Mama's endless fatigue.

A few days after my father left, Beni asked me what war was. I said that I wasn't exactly sure but there were men in town with medals who would talk on holidays about glory and country. And then there were all the others who didn't understand that kind of glory or didn't want it.

"Why did Mama say there's a war between Fabian and Zsabo?" my brother asked.

"That's a different kind of war," Mama replied. "A private war between neighbors when one family's animal wanders onto the pasture of the other, and they argue, they take revenge on each other, the hate is passed from father to son. But that's a war only in a manner of speaking. This war is being waged by a man who wants to take over the whole world—that madman with the mustache who took all the Jews from our town, took all the Roma, and one day, you'll see it will happen to us, too."



"But we aren't Roma or Jews," I said. "Why would he take us away?"

"Even Christ was Jewish," my mother replied. She wouldn't say any more.

The war went on. From Papa, after a yellow post-card stamped "combat zone," we had no more news. The townspeople were sick with sadness and hunger. Every so often there came a message of a husband or son who had done his duty for the Fatherland. We all now knew clearly what those words meant. And people despaired, blaming the devil with the mustache, the evil spirit, the man with the foreign name. We were called down to the town hall in shifts every day to hand over cattle, gold, foodstuffs. A town crier made the rounds, saying we had to give everything for the Nation: "For the Nation that's bleeding and suffering."

Sometimes, my mother would tell me her horrible dreams; they were almost always of men marching through blood or crossing a river of red, and when they came closer, she saw that they had no legs.

"Was Papa there, too?" Beni asked.

"Don't talk that way, Mama," I said. "The dreams

mean nothing. You said once yourself that red blood means hope."

"But that blood was black," Mama replied, "and it means mourning."

By then, we were eating what little grew in the yard, and Mama ate less and less to leave more for us.

One day, we were told to go to the town hall because there was a letter along with a package for us. "It must be from Papa. Maybe he sent us something to eat!" I shouted, jumping for joy. But Mama stopped me cold with a voice that seemed to come from the other world.

"Be quiet." And my heart grew even smaller.

Without telling Mama, I went to get the package. I was sent away with a form to sign. I returned home with the document and Mama signed it without reading it; the form was something official and I thought nothing of it. After I brought the letter and the package home, I wanted to open them but Mama said it wasn't urgent. I said it was best to open it right away because it might contain food; it wasn't the first time that soldiers had sent some home. Mama grabbed hold of the oil lamp and in a calm voice I'd never heard her use before, she told us to gather round.

There were just a few lines, typewritten; there was a small red cross on the envelope, like on the sheet of paper. I thought it came from a hospital and I asked Mama if Papa was sick or wounded but she didn't answer. She folded the letter, and after putting it under her pillow without reading what it said to us, she told me to open the package.

I cut the twine quickly and dumped what was inside onto the floor.

"Papa's laundry!" I exclaimed. "Socks, underpants—and all full of lice. Why, Mama? Who sent the package? Tell me, Mama."

"Burn all of it, hurry," Mama said. "Lice are quick to suck blood."

In the same calm voice, Mama kept repeating, "Watch out for the lice."

While I burned Papa's underwear, I noticed Mama slowly lay her head on the pillow and close her eyes.

In a low voice, I told Beni that Mama was asleep and when she woke up, she would get a surprise. . . . I'd managed to get two eggs from our neighbors, and I would make the bean and potato soup that she liked so much.

"Get a tray ready for the soup," Beni suggested to me, "and put it with soft-boiled eggs, the way she likes them, and a white napkin."

It was a shame to wake her; it seemed like she was really resting for the first time. She'd never spent a day in bed her whole life; even on Sundays, she sewed and washed our patched, threadbare clothes until sundown. But we needed to wake her to know what the letter said.

"You wake her," I murmured to Beni. "She gets angry with me more easily."

"No, it's better if you do it," he said, "since you're head of the family. And besides, she admires you, while I don't count for much."

"If I'm head of the family, then I order you to wake her up."

"But she's sleeping so peacefully," Beni said. "I hate to wake her."

"OK, come here. We'll draw lots."

With one hand, I took a bean, and without needing to hide it, I balled up my fists under Beni's hands and asked him to guess. He guessed right.

"Good! Call her."

"Mama, dinner is ready and look what we have," Beni said. He repeated "Mama" louder. "Open your eyes and you won't believe what you see." To me, he said, "Why is she in such a deep sleep? She always used to wake up at the littlest thing."

"She's so tired," I replied. "Call her again! Maybe she's pretending to sleep so she can leave the food for us, and she'll skip dinner."

I brought the tray to the bed and I lifted the ladle to Mama's nose. "Mama, do you notice this wonderful aroma? And how warm it is?" The steam from the soup beaded on her face.

"Mama!" we both yelled suddenly in unison. "Mama! Mama!"

The tray fell to the floor, the plates shattered. Beni searched for Mama's hands. When he found them, he let out a frightened cry. "She's cold! She's dead! Dead, Lenke, Mama is dead! Lenke, where are you?"

"I'm here," I replied. I leaned on Beni who was trembling like a leaf, and I felt myself sinking into the darkness. My strength drained away and my flesh ached.

"The letter, Lenke," Beni shouted. "Papa, too."

"Yes," I replied, "it's just the two of us."

"You promised me to go to the doctor, remember? You said you would never leave me, remember? You have to take me to the city. Lenke, answer me." My brother kept talking. He was hot and trembled with fever.



A carpenter who was a bit feeble-minded made the casket out of fir wood that oozed sap. The neighbors helped me wash and dress my mother. I found four older men among the townspeople and asked them to carry Mama to the graveyard. They walked with difficulty on the slippery patches of snow. I couldn't cry; Beni sobbed endlessly. The snow crunched underfoot like sugar; I told Beni so I had something to say. At that moment, planes passed over us and we heard explosions. The cemetery was empty of flowers and crosses. There was nothing there except us and a couple of dogs digging in the ground to find below what they could no longer find above. They howled up at the sky and yelped for a long time.

When we returned from the graveyard, I decided to throw one of our four chairs into the wood stove. We now only needed two of them and we could feel the cold in our bones.

"What chair are you putting in the fire?" Beni asked. "Not Mama's and not Papa's, either, although we have to put in something."

"Let's put in the chair that wobbles," I said.

"The one she'd sit on while sewing outside during

the summer?" Beni retorted. "Oh no. She always sat on that one so she wouldn't ruin the others, remember?"

We argued a long time over the choice; all four of them reminded us of something, and in the end, we decided to draw lots. Beni won again.

"Take four steps," I said, "and we'll burn the one you bump into first."

"This one!" Beni exclaimed. "Which one is it?"

"It's the chair where Mama sewed but it's also the one that's lost all its varnish so it won't smell so much as it burns."

That winter was the longest of my life. Slowly, I burned everything we had, along with my memories. But Mama's bed we left alone. I hadn't touched it since that day. I couldn't bring myself to cover it or remove the sheets; leaving it gave the illusion that she would come back one day. When she closed her eyes never to open them again, her death was more human than her life had been.

One day Beni asked me, "Do we have any more furniture?"

"Yes," I said. "The bed, the wardrobe . . . And there's always the house. After the war, we'll sell everything and with the money, I'll take you to the city to see the doctor. No one is buying now. Who would want a house that could fall apart from age or be destroyed in a bombing?"

"We needed the clock," Beni said with a sigh, "so we could check the time for the train."

"It would be nice to have, it's true. But nothing is worth anything anymore."

The war was never-ending. Our windows were covered with black paper, which was torn in many places. The window panes were broken, too, and along with the light they let in a freezing wind.

Then suddenly it was springtime and we felt hopeful again about life. People brought us food, leaving it at our door, without ever coming in. Mama's wedding linens ended up going for flour and milk and sugar, and all that remained was the velvet bedspread, and the drapes, which I wished to sell after the war. I decided I would begin working in the fields during the summer; I'd bring Beni along, and the plan revived us.

Before summer arrived, two uniformed men came looking for us at dawn. "It must be something about Papa," I thought. "They must be soldiers he fought with, or else, who knows what." I looked out the window: there were two gendarmes, and a foreigner in a darker uniform. This last man, after greeting the officers, pointed to our house. I opened the window to hear what they were saying.

"This will be quick," the tall one said. "There are only four left. You go on ahead and I'll see you at the station." They parted with the words, "Heil Hitler!"

I remembered this greeting because Mama felt sick every time she heard it. Now I understood everything: there had also been Jews in our family—two of my father's cousins whom we only saw on certain occasions. They went to synagogue just like we went to church.

I jumped out of bed and told Beni to get dressed. "Quick! We're going to take the train to the city."

"What?" he said. "Why now?"

"Hurry," I said. "There's a train leaving soon . . . I think some men are coming to collect us. Did you think the world had forgotten about us? We'll bring the velvet quilt and the drapes. People in the city have money."

"I'm afraid," Beni said. "The darkness is inside me, too."

"That's silly, Benike," I said. "It's still a bit dark outside. That's why you feel more darkness."

A gendarme came to the door, and knocked hard.

"I'm coming," I shouted. "We're ready."

"That's what I like. Obedient, orderly children," he replied. Then turning to the other official, he said, "They'll cooperate."

"Take my hand and don't let go until I tell you," I said to Beni. "This man thinks you're afraid of the doctor, but you mustn't be afraid of anything."

On the way, a few farmers tried to talk to us or give us something; one made to hold out some bread but then froze midway because he didn't dare.

A toothless old woman approached me, laughing.

"I used to know your great-grandfather," she said. "An old swindler who traded in feathers. He would come to see me often when he passed this way."

But one of the gendarmes shoved her away. Beni asked me again why these men were helping us. "Because we're orphans," I replied. "Because Papa died in the war. There are a lot of people in need of help and they don't want it widely known, otherwise they wouldn't even be able to do this. That's why they're acting rude and annoyed."

"I don't like their voices," Beni said. "I'd like to leave some other time. Listen, let's go back home."

"We're already at the station. If you could see how grand the train is. So long!"



A gendarme came over and shoved me hard in the back, driving Beni and me inside the crowded train car where people were wailing.

"Why is everyone moaning?" my brother asked.

"You're not the only one who's sick here," I replied. "They're taking the sickest people to get healed."

"What kind of people are there on this train? Why are there men shouting?" Beni kept overwhelming me with questions.

"We can't travel in comfort. There's a war on, and Hungary is poor. You have to remember that, Beni. If you want, I can tell you what the train is like . . ."

I was shoved and kicked by the gendarmes who were imposing order and putting a stop to the wailing. I shielded Beni but was clutching my side because of a terrible blow I'd taken. Fear and sorrow seeped into my bones along with the cold, and I was afraid it would be impossible to find lies big enough to hide all that was happening from Beni.

"So, the train car is nicely furnished," I said with effort. "There are plenty of red velvet seats and lovely white curtains. The people are well-dressed and all look very nice but they are weak—some are suffering even more than you. There's a woman eating chocolate, I can ask her for a piece if you want, though I'd prefer to wait until we get to the city and I can buy it for you myself."

"Oh, Lenke, I don't feel well," Beni kept saying. "This darkness will never end, I know it."

"You're just like Mama," I said. "You feel everything. But what's about to happen, you can't feel—you must simply believe me. . . . Hug me and hold onto me with all of your might. We'll wake up in a new world. I can already see the first lights of the city."

## *Silvia*

WE WERE LIVING in a small city called Bamberg, not far from Nuremberg, when my father left us after a few days of furlough, which he'd more than earned through his excellent performance as a senior officer in the Third Reich. I don't recall the pleasure of long visits with my father in those days, and I never saw him out of his pristine uniform, which so thrilled my mother.

I never counted for much in our household, and even less since my brother had received Father's permission to join the Hitler Youth. After that, the pride Mama felt as a wife and mother was boundless.

We were a well-known and admired family in our small city, and at church on Sundays, everyone paid their respects to the Schultz family. I was the only one who felt embarrassed, useless as I was between such big, strong men like my father and my brother, both of whom walked with precise, firm strides, as if a beat only they could hear moved them from within. No matter how hard I tried, I could never stay in step with them and had to run to catch up, like a lamb that had been separated from its flock. They pointed to my brother as an example, always telling me that I didn't have the right spring in my step.

On the rare occasions we were all together, my mother would take the long way to church, seeking out routes where people would bow and greet us warmly. "You're almost twelve now, but you just don't want to grow up," my mother said to me. "Look at Mrs. Hass's son. He's your age but you look like his little brother."



I wished my father and brother could remain at home with us. When I saw them happily leaving for the front, it felt like they didn't love me. My mother, tall and bony, was submissive by nature: when we brought them to the station, one look from my father was enough to make her swallow her tears. My mother was strong, though, and on nights when she couldn't sleep, she'd clean the floors or polish the silver that she kept in two large suitcases on top of the wardrobe in her bedroom.

"Why don't you let Hilde help you?" I would ask. I thought she was trying to save our elderly housekeeper the trouble. She was the only servant who'd remained with us during the war years.

"She's tired, the poor thing," my mother replied. "I can do it myself. Besides, I'm not tired. . . ."

"Why are you putting that stuff away? Are we leaving, too?"

"Robert, we're at war. Anything can happen in the blink of an eye. Even having to save our most precious things."

"Tell me about the war," I said to my mother. "Something that's real, not a fairy tale. When we're alone, you treat me like a little child. You're the one who makes me feel younger than my age."

"There are duties in life," my mother replied. "Duties for men. And when you're older, you won't fail to carry out your duty."

"What duties?"

"You must love country above all else. You must be proud of your father and your brother and not whimper every time they have to leave, hanging on your father's neck like a sack of potatoes. The love between us is strong, but it's the hope of winning that gives us the strength to be apart. The War isn't just glory—the glory has to be earned. And we will earn it, Robert!"

"I wish you would sleep next to me, Mama, when I hear the planes overhead at night. I never told anyone that I'm scared because none of you seem scared."

"You're a big boy now, Robert," she said. But that night Mother slid into bed beside me. It was one of the happy moments of my childhood, like when I played chess with my father and my mother whispered to him that he should let me win at least once. He got mad, insisting that glory had to be earned and that winning took desire and willpower.

"You're right, Papa," I said. That made my father's

blue eyes light up and he began stroking his thick brown hair, which he wore parted down the middle. He was short and muscular, with light skin, rosy cheeks, and squat hands. Once Mother dared to raise her voice at him, calling him a peasant, then falling into a deep silence to emphasize her own aristocratic origins.



Our house was spacious and no one slept upstairs; since the war broke out, we'd all settled on the ground floor so that if the sirens went off it would be easier to reach the bunker my father had had built out back by the garden. My toys were still all lined up in my room on the upper floor but I rarely went up there because the warren of long-abandoned rooms frightened me and made me sad. I didn't really feel like playing anymore anyway, so for fun after school, I would go to the railroad crossing to watch the trains and later draw them at home.

I loved walking along the tracks, waving at the traveling strangers. I often hid in the woods near the tracks and made snowballs to throw at the train cars, hoping to hit the windows. Some people laughed, some got mad. These trains never stopped at the signal master's station. But one time someone complained, and Mother locked me in Hilde's quarters; a tiny dark room with an iron-frame cot, where I eventually fell asleep. She didn't let me out until the next day, so Hilde was forced to spend the night in the kitchen sitting by the stove, grumbling more than usual that she was a burden to everyone. She prayed that she would die soon, all the more since my mother had developed insomnia and started rising in the middle of the night to clean the floors.

It'd been the signalman who ratted me out, so I learned to stay clear of him and hide better in the woods, where I felt like master of the tracks and could observe the little white station house at the railroad crossing and the water well. One day I was trying to balance on a rail as usual, when I felt the tracks vibrate beneath my feet as if a train were coming. I didn't see any lights or signals, or hear the warning whistle, yet I was sure a train was approaching. It was a dark, foggy afternoon, and I stepped away just in time to see a black transport train pulled by two locomotives come to a stop at the signalman's station. I threw myself into the snow and looked up to see a train car door opened by an armed soldier. Two men exited carrying a pail in each hand while the soldier pushed them with the butt of his rifle, saying, "*Schnell! Schnell!*"



From a distance, the soldier looked like my father, and I ran out from the woods to get a better look. The man was stocky and he wore the same black uniform. I couldn't make out his face, but his walk and bearing made me call out, "Papa! Papa!" as I jumped up and down, sinking into the snow.

"Go home!" the signal master shouted as the soldier who resembled but was not my father grabbed me by the arm and pushed me toward the woods, cursing. I wound up neck-deep in the snow, but still, I couldn't take my eyes off the train car, all those arms sticking through the window grates and the voices from inside of men, women, and children, crying out and begging: "*Bitteschön*," they said again and again. "*Wasser, wasser, bitte*."

The snowball remained in my fist but I couldn't feel the cold. I considered throwing it at one of the windows for a second, but then I hesitated and the train moved on, slowly disappearing into the fog.

All alone, I could hear those voices buzzing in my ears, growing louder, fearfully doubling in intensity like a collective wail and I felt my wet hands burning. I was ashamed for not throwing the snowball as I had the other times. I stumbled out of the hole and started off for home, mumbling, "Mama . . . Mama . . ."

When I arrived, I no longer wanted to see anyone, not even my mother, and I snuck in like a thief.

"Is that you, Robert?" my mother asked from the kitchen.

Standing in the middle of the living room, I had one thought only: to hide behind a piece of furniture. The voices still echoed in my head, begging, "Water, water."

"Robert, look at the puddle!" my mother yelled. "You're getting my rug all wet. Your shoes are covered in snow and look at your hands. My God, what a state you're in!"

My mother removed my wet clothes and Hilde fetched a hot water bottle and a wool blanket. They put me to bed where I lay delirious the whole night. They watched over me for several days but dodged my questions on the truth about the train. Mother reacted severely, threatening to slap me and report it all to my father, alternating her threats with entreaties and kisses. My mother wore pants, because of the cold, she said, and because in wartime it didn't matter how one dressed, but to me she seemed harsh like a man. I could hardly bear it, so I decided to escape.



One morning, I jumped out of the window into the snow covering the yard and instinctively began running to the signalman's station. The guard was asleep on a cot. He wore a green uniform that was different from my father's and he had a rifle propped up against his large belly, which rose and fell as he snored. I stood there staring at him for a long time, holding my breath out of fear that I'd wake him, preferring he wake up on his own. Eventually he did, and, shaking himself, he shot up off of the cot and grabbed the rifle.

"Who goes there?" he shouted.

"I'm Colonel Schultz's son," I said.

He didn't relax, even when he realized I was just a child.

"I've already chased you off once, so what the devil are you doing back here?"

"I want to know who those passengers were."

He looked at me with hostility, then sat down, but this time he leaned the rifle against the wall.

"I don't know anything," the signalman said. "I do my duty, whatever my superiors like your father order me to do. I am an honorable soldier, I follow orders . . ."

I interrupted his remarks. "Are you a soldier or the station master?"

"I'm a railway worker in soldier's uniform. I always

wanted to be station master and now that they've built this shed, the only trains that come through here are those cursed trains. . . . They've turned my home into a latrine!"

He spit out the cigarette butt, which had been hanging extinguished on his lower lip, along with brown jets of saliva.

Then he began again: "If you could smell the stench! At my age they're still making me serve, but I would prefer the front to burying the shit from these vermin, which I have to do twice a day. What a disgrace!"



"So two trains come a day?"

I must have looked at him with apprehension because he responded immediately: "That's when I bury it, but there are many other trains." Then he remembered himself. "Go home instead of asking all these stupid questions. I'm a soldier and I'm ordering you to stay away from here for good. Understood? Now *marsch*."

Suddenly there was the sound of a train outside and, jumping to his feet, the signalman grabbed his rifle and opened the door. He had me go out first, pushing me with a little shove. But instead of going home, I ran back to my spot in the woods and watched the same scene as the day before. This time there were two armed soldiers, one of whom stood by the window, poking with his bayonet at the hands reaching out in search of water.

I scooped up some snow and rolled it into balls, throwing them against the barred windows of another train car that wasn't being patrolled. But the guard noticed, and raised his rifle in my direction. He took a few shots, sending me tumbling down the snowy slope. Trembling with fear, I crouched there for a long time with my face and body half-buried in the snow, unable to move. It seemed as though it wasn't only the train wailing, but the whole forest. When I finally lifted my head, the train had left but the sobbing continued, fainter now and closer to me. Was I the one crying? I touched my cheeks—wet, but I didn't know whether from tears or snow—then I set off into the utter silence of the woods. The groans began again, even fainter but real. I went in the direction the voice seemed to be coming from, and as I ran, I tripped over a mound of snow; the weeping was coming from underneath.

"Who's there?" I shouted.

No one answered, but the snowy little mound moved and I saw a slender arm laboring to poke out, followed by one tiny hand waving, then another. I bent down to touch the arms and to shake them with all of my strength just to be sure this wasn't a nightmare. Digging frantically, I found a little girl wrapped in a coat that, like her hair and eyelashes, was covered in icy snow. I wiped her face, but her frozen tears were like drops of candle wax and they wouldn't budge. I helped her stand up, and removing my coat, scarf, and gloves, I covered her with my clothes. This pretty little girl who was somehow still alive just stared at me, wide-eyed.

"What's your name?" I asked her. "Where are you from? Who are you? Why aren't you saying anything?"

She stood there stiffly, without moving. I began rubbing her arms and warming her face and hands with my breath.

"Come with me," I said. "Come home with me. I have to go because my mother is waiting for me."

She began looking around, her eyes tearing up, but she didn't say anything. I picked her up and held her in my arms; she was as light as a feather, my coat weighed more than her. I wasn't strong enough to carry her all the way to our house; I could feel my heart pounding while my teeth chattered from the cold. Before placing her back on the ground, I smiled and explained we still had a bit farther to walk. Only a few more steps, I said, and we would be somewhere warm.

She looked at me, frightened. Worried she'd try to escape, I took her hand and I pulled her along the icy path. She tried to break away, but the sudden movement and the heaviness of the two coats on top of her made her fall on the ice. As I tried lifting her up again, I heard my mother's voice and then Hilde's. They were looking for me.

"We're here," I yelled. "Come quick, Mama!"

When my mother saw the girl, she went pale and seemed about to faint.

"Robert," she said, her voice weak, "who is this child wearing your clothes?"

"I don't know," I replied. "I found her in the woods. She hasn't said a word. Maybe she's mute."

"You've gone insane," she shouted. "Do you want to ruin your father and our whole family? Come in the house, we have to hide, quick."

As she spoke, her trembling hands unbuttoned the two coats the girl was wearing but opening the first was enough to reveal what she was looking for. With a sudden motion, she tore off the yellow star that was sewn on the girl's tiny overcoat, and before I could protest, she crumpled up the yellow piece of fabric and dug a hole in the snow with her heel. She buried the star, then stomped on the snow for what seemed like forever. It was as if she were a dog burying its waste. It was so ridiculous I almost felt like laughing.

"You always wanted a girl," I said to Mother, who stared at me without moving. "Here's a daughter for you and a little sister for me."

"Oh, Robert . . . Robert . . ." my mother said under her breath. Then she burst into tears.

We were in the house, in my room, next to my bed where I'd decided the girl should rest. Hilde was going back and forth from the kitchen, refilling the hot water bottle and bringing broth and conserved fruit. I begged my mother to feed her, to spoon something into her mouth, but she seemed absent, too, so I began helping Hilde, who grumbled, but in an unusually kind voice.

A spoonful at a time, Hilde fed the girl, who now appeared to be smiling at me while she swallowed faster and faster. Meanwhile, I explained how and where I'd found the girl, adding that she couldn't be mute because I'd heard her wailing just as I'd heard the people on the train.

"She needs a doctor," I kept saying. "She's not mute, she's sick. We need to help her talk. Isn't that right, Hilde?"

"The young lady will be our special guest, if that's what you wish," replied Hilde, still grumbling.

That evening, I was as happy as if I'd discovered a gold mine. Even Hilde seemed more energetic. Mother was the only one who couldn't understand. Suddenly she jerked me away from the bed, yelling, "Get away from her! Don't touch that animal!"

"You mustn't talk that way, Mama," I replied. "She's little. Can't you see she's already fallen asleep? You always said you wanted a little girl named Silvia. From now on, we'll call her Silvia."

Leaning over the bed where Silvia slept, I pronounced loudly, "In the name of the Father, the Son, and the Holy Spirit, I baptize you Silvia Schultz."

"You're out of your mind," Mama said, hysterical. "Do as you please. Have your little toy. But when your father comes home. . . ."

After that, I stopped going to the signal master's station, and I no longer heard the wails echoing in my head. I grew ever fonder of Silvia as she learned to say a few words in German, but she couldn't—or wouldn't—express herself otherwise. It seemed like she had forgotten her language. She had become quite pretty and lively; she knew how to write her numbers from one to ten, and she'd even confided in me her age:

she was six. We played all day in the room upstairs, which I'd reopened after she arrived. We slept there in twin beds and I even convinced Mother to wish Silvia goodnight. But we weren't allowed out of the house; I'd promised as much to Mama so she would be kind and considerate to Silvia. There was nothing, however, that I could do about the disgust my mother felt when she touched Silvia. In fact, Hilde was the one who dressed her every day and put her to bed at night.

After a while, Silvia began walking around the house by herself. Every now and then, she would stop to touch a piece of furniture or an object, almost as if she were looking for something. She stroked Mama's furs, burying her little hands inside of them. She tried one on, running to the mirror to see how she looked.

"Tell her to stop," my mother said. "She's ruining my furs. She's making them dirty."

"Why don't you tell her yourself?" I would say. "She understands everything."

My little sister was plumping up nicely, and every so often a quick smile would flash across her chubby cheeks. But at night, when she was alone with me, she often cried and I would console her. Once she hugged me and gave me a kiss in front of my mother.

"Give Mama a kiss, too," I said to Silvia.

My mother stiffened and looked at the child with contempt, but she didn't move. Then, putting on her fur coat, she said she had to go to the post office to send a telegram to Father. I ran after her and at the door, I said, "Silvia must stay with us until the war is over. Then we'll look for her parents."

"If you can find them," my mother replied in a strange tone.

A few days later, my father returned from the front.

"You had to call for me now, just when they need me most? With the Russians and the Americans closing in on the Reich?" he said.

Mama clearly hadn't found the courage to tell him the real reason for the telegram.

He didn't appear to have noticed Silvia, who stood in a corner of the room, frightened, her eyes coldly trained on my father's boots.

"The rug, dear," said my mother, also staring at his boots, so covered in melting snow that two dark water stains had begun spreading across the rug.

My father looked up, his gaze traveling to where Silvia stood staring at him. Both my mother's eyes and mine were glued to the carpet where the stains were growing larger.

"Who is that child?" he said in a serious voice. "Speak!" he shouted. "What's happening in my house, Grete? Is this turning into a synagogue? A dump? A scrap heap?"

"I found her," I said to Father, who seemed intent on thrashing my mother. "She was in the woods, near the railway where you see the trains—those trains that . . ."

He struck me before I could finish, sending me flying across the room to where Silvia stood, petrified like a rabbit facing a hunter's rifle. I took her hand; her whole body was trembling.

"Don't touch her, Papa," I said, in tears. "You're not her father. Beat me instead."

He raised his hand to hit me again, but Mother came between us and he unloaded all of his rage upon her, beating her savagely.

"Forgive me," my mother begged, "if we had taken her away from him, we would have lost Robert—maybe forever. Please, calm down, Fritz. Let's try to be reasonable."

"Did you know she was Jewish or not?" my father asked, speaking in a calm tone again.

"Of course I knew," Mama replied. "I knew as soon as I saw them walking out of the woods together, even before I got rid of the yellow star. Who else would be in the woods? They must have lost her, or her parents pushed her off the train to save her. But she doesn't speak . . ."

My father motioned to the child to come closer, but Silvia didn't move.

"You two go upstairs," he said to Mother and me. Turning to Hilde, he said, "You stay in the kitchen."

Mother and I stood outside the door motionless, waiting anxiously.

I could hear my father interrogating Silvia, demanding her name, age, and hometown, as if she were a soldier.

"Are you Polish? Hungarian? Romanian?" he asked angrily. "Which train brought you?"

"I don't remember," she muttered.

"You must remember and answer me fully if you want to see your parents again. Speak!"

After an unbearable silence, my father's voice exploded in the air. "What, have you lost your tongue? May the devil take you!" shouted Father. "Follow me, I'm going to send you to the same place as your parents!"

The door was suddenly thrown open and my father appeared, holding Silvia by the collar of her dress. She hung in the air like a kitten.

"I don't remember," Silvia kept saying.

"I'm taking you to the bunker and your memory will come back by tomorrow morning."

I threw myself against my father. "I'll report you!" I shouted. "You'll never see me again."

He dragged her to the bunker and then immediately came back, smiling. His anger appeared to have disappeared completely. He looked at us almost tenderly now that the source of tension was no longer right in front of his eyes. I understood he wanted to forget about it for the moment and was trying to be accommodating with my mother and me.

"Grete, get me the chess set," my father said. "Come on Robert, let's see who'll win. Defend yourself well."

He gazed at me, offering a challenge but with a touch of admiration because, for the first time, my will to win was equal to his. Mother poured him a glass of cognac and sat down on a chair next to us, not to watch our match as she normally would but to read the newspapers my father had brought.

I had to win. I gave the game everything I had, as if Silvia's life depended on it.

“Fritz,” my mother said, after a long silence, “don’t you have any news about Helmuth? Now that his regiment is back in Germany, couldn’t he perhaps come home? He is after all just a boy. . . .”

“You want him to come home now? Are you giving up, too?” my father replied, without looking away from the chess board. After a moment, he said, “Did you put provisions in the bunker?”



Hearing my mother assure him she had, I was secretly happy for Silvia.

That night, I went back to sleeping in my own room after a long absence. I felt at ease there because Silvia was safe and my father was home with us. I fell asleep quickly, filled with the satisfaction that I had beaten my father at chess.

I had a terrible dream; it was as though the earth trembled, shaking my bed and causing the trees in the woods to fall, blocking the train tracks. Even my window buckled, and a strong blast shattered the glass. I woke up with a start. Through the wide-open window, I could see the dark sky, and a deafening noise made me feel disoriented. Jumping out of bed, I yelled, “Papa!” Just then, a sudden flash blinded me and the room was plunged into darkness.

When I came to again, I heard loud banging on the wall. A lot of time must have gone by, and I was no longer sure where I was. A weak light entered the room, filtered by a tangle of ceiling beams and debris from the broken wall plaster. A mechanical-sounding voice, speaking in a foreign language, resounded at intervals, repeating the same words. I wanted to move, but I was trapped by something that squeezed my legs with a jaw-like grip. Confused, I began crying and yelling for help. I started clawing my way out of the rubble of bricks and dust where I must have fallen. The banging on the wall began again, with the sound sometimes close, sometimes far. I could hear the picks and the shovels at work and the foreign voices that seemed to guide them. Finally, the sky above me opened up and I saw a pair of heads and then two soldiers in uniform and a man in a white coat. They were talking to me but I could only understand their gestures and encouraging smiles. The man with the white coat was the first to lean into the opening and after he freed me from the rubble, he took me in his arms and emerged into the light of the sun.



For a lingering moment, I was practically blind. My eyes were wide open now but they refused to see: in front of me, there was only smoke and debris, my house had been swallowed up by a crater of ashes and all around me were voices coming through loudspeakers and sirens from Red Cross vehicles. I babbled, "Where am I? Mama? Mama?"

Through the many incomprehensible voices talking over each other and giving what sounded like orders, I heard someone call me, "Robert!"

I turned around, and in front of the bunker, which was unscathed except for the torn-off door, I saw Silvia, who ran toward me holding the hand of a young nurse.

Silvia had a sign hanging around her neck that read: "Miryam Lewy, Born 1939, Budapest."

Breathless, I looked at her closely to make sure it was really Silvia, pointing questioningly at the sign.

"It's me, Robert! It's me," Silvia assured me.

"Where's Mother?" I yelled, sobbing. Then lowering my voice instinctively, I asked, "And where's Father? Where are they?"



"I was found in the bunker," Silvia said. "I was alone."

"Where are they?" I shouted. "I want to look for them."

I thought about breaking free from the arms of the stranger who held me. Looking alternately at me, then at Silvia, the soldiers and the nurse were arguing. I began trembling with fear. I was afraid of everything and everyone and I couldn't manage to say my name even as the nurse, holding a blank card and a pencil, asked me yet another time.

"What is your name?" the foreign woman said in English.

I looked at Silvia, silently imploring her for help. She removed the sign from her neck, asked the nurse for a pencil, then she crossed out her name and changed it to Silvia. Now all of them were laughing, amused, and she smiled, too, looking at me sweetly.

"Your name? Your name?" the young woman kept repeating in English as she walked us toward the Red Cross vehicle.

Silvia answered for me: "Robert."

"Robert? Robert, only Robert?" The nurse handed me a piece of chocolate and waited for my answer.

"Robert Lewy," Silvia replied, smiling. Then she turned to me and said in German, "You're my brother, right?"

# *A Surprise*

On one side of the dam there were a few small, low-slung houses, and on the other a forest so long and narrow you could see the river lazily rolling by behind it on bright, sunny days. Twice a year, the farmers jumped into the yellow river with horses and cows that had scabby crusts to wash. The men waded in wearing long underwear and the women were almost completely dressed because no one dared face the town's disapproval over an issue of morality.

We were living down at the end of the main road, 48 Brinka Street. The houses didn't clearly advance up to No. 48 and on the day that I decided to count them, I discovered there were thirty-nine in all, including the school and town hall. I asked my mother why there were more addresses than buildings and I learned that, many years before, when the dam wasn't there to protect us, about a third of the town had been washed away by the river as it raged.

After that, the villagers battled town officials for years until they built the dam as an embankment for the river and also the main thoroughfare for the whole town. On Sundays, you could see the rich and the poor as they went to mass. They paraded by in proper order: first Baron Radozy and his family, flanked on either side by the veterinarian and the schoolmaster, then in the second row were the gendarmes and the town's two employees who were fairly popular. Their clout had grown since the day when there appeared at town hall a massive, black, shiny typewriter that they used to type, with a single finger, the villagers' births and deaths. They also knew how to write in longhand, but that was little wonder to us children who went to school. After the town leaders came painted carriages, and the most beautiful horses in the world trotted by, led by their masters, rich landowners who possessed stretches of the woods where they could hunt. The peasants followed behind, and lastly came the simpletons, amid the kids' laughter and pranks.



I watched them walk by, knowing them all, rich and poor, and I waved to them as if at a show, even if few waved back.

The locals spoke a dialect mixed with Slovenian and Russian but the official language was Hungarian because in those years our province was still part of Hungary.

I was happy living in our town, but I didn't enjoy going to our cold, damp school, especially after they substituted someone else for our beloved teacher, who was always coughing—which perhaps was why he had to leave. Every time he said my name, he collapsed in a coughing fit. I don't know where my long and difficult name came from, but for my old teacher it was agony saying, "Let me call on . . . Gugorovitschinsky!"

He never wanted to call me simply Melinka; he often said, "In life, only your family name counts."

And so, for two years, I was almost always left alone.



The new teacher didn't love my last name either, but boy did he know how to say it! During class, he never let go of his leather riding crop, just as after school he was never without his hunting rifle. His name was Attila and we easily found a nickname for him. From the very first day, he was Mr. Scourge. He had more interest in wild game than in school and our only hope was that he'd leave the town he hated with all of his being. Naturally, his dislike included us school children. One day, he said to me, "Your name isn't worthy of a Christian."

The whole class laughed.

"I'm not Christian, Mr. Scourge," I said.

"Silence! No joking," he yelled. "I'm not one to be fooled. I can spot a Jew from a kilometer away."

A murmur rose from the class while the teacher looked me over, and said, "No, you have nothing to do with that race."

"I think I do," I stammered. And just as I'd stood up, I automatically sat down.

"Stand up!" he shouted again. "I'm not done speaking to you."

I remained standing in that spot for the whole lesson. Out on the street, my friends kept asking, "What did you say that we couldn't hear?" and "If you did nothing wrong, why did he punish you?"

"I don't know," I replied, "it's not my fault."

At home, where I relayed everything, my mother also looked at me suspiciously.

"If you must run your mouth, I'd prefer you do so with me. School is essential—ask your father who only finished the third grade. How far has he gone in life? As far as selling needles, buttons, and thread house to house. But needles last a long time, thread is needed less and less now that people buy their clothes already made, and as for buttons, we have a closet full of them and we'll end up eating them because no one wants them."

I laughed at the thought of eating buttons. My mother, who rarely appreciated my sense of humor, took advantage by placing a piece of paper and an envelope before me to dictate a letter to family in Prague. Along with greetings from my mother, Arina, my father, Karl, my grandmother, and the four of us nieces and nephews, and the habitual invitation, which was repeated every year at Passover, to come visit while Grandmother was still alive, my mother wished to make a specific request in the letter for four pairs of underwear all made of wool but in different sizes. In our neck of the woods, the only children who wore underwear were Jewish. I knew this because at school my friends and I had talked about it a lot; on

Sundays out on the avenue, when the boys harassed the slow-witted girls by lifting their petticoats, I'd noticed they had nothing on underneath either.

So I said to my mother: "My friends already call me 'miss' because I wear underpants. If the ones I have on fall apart, I'll go around like all the other girls."

"You're not a farm girl," my mother replied, "but if it were up to you, you'd follow them into church nude. May I ask why you go? I haven't seen any of your friends at the synagogue."



"Well, of course not."

"And why not?" my mother shot back. "Isn't it the same as you going to church with them? Try inviting them to temple and see what kind of faces they make."

"You always go too far, Mama. They are kind and helpful. Besides, who lights and extinguishes the lamps on Saturdays? Who fetches the goulash and baked beans for us? For us Jews, everything is forbidden."

"They don't do it for free," Mama said. "I always give them a piece of cake or a button or even some money, when we have it. Don't worry, they don't do it for free."

During recess at school the next day, I asked my best friend, "Want to come to the synagogue with me on Saturday?"

"How much will you pay me?" she replied.

I said nothing but from that day forward, my appreciation for my mother grew.

Passover came early that year and the snow on top of the roof hadn't melted yet. It's one reason why I remember it but not the main one. The second reason is that Christians and Jews celebrate Easter and Passover at almost the same time. And for once our holiday breaks coincided.

The third reason is the most surprising, and it's worth telling. I was coming home from the last day of school when I saw a group of well-dressed people on Brinka Street, craning their necks as they searched for an address. Counting both men and women, there were fifteen of them, give or take.

"That's too many people to be coming from the tax collector's office," I thought to myself. Besides, I knew the tax collectors. They'd always arrived in twos, all the times they had come to take inventory of our house!

These people, instead, were foreigners who were looking for a dead person's house. I followed them for a while and when I was absolutely certain the address they were looking for was ours, I ran ahead to let my mother know we had guests. I bumped into my grandmother, who was seated as usual outside of our front door in her winter woolen shawl, as if waiting for who knows what.

"Can't you see? Are you blind?" my grandmother said testily.

"Can't you see, Grandma?" I said. "Look at all these people coming to our house. Who are they?"

"Where? Where are they?" She tried to get to her feet but her legs were even feebler than her eyes.

When the crowd of people had reached our house, Grandmother let out such a shout that my mother nearly fainted out of fright. She ran from the kitchen and stood for a moment on the threshold as if turned to stone, holding a knife she'd been using to peel potatoes. Then she joined the visitors who were clinging to Grandma like fruit to a tree.

Worried, I said, "What's happening?"

Mama wasn't listening to me, and it seemed as though her voice was suddenly unearthing an infinite number of names.



"Boriska!" she was shouting. "Fanny! Helen! Oh Sholem! And you, Irenke! My brothers and sisters! Moshe! David! Marek! Ivan! Ferenc! Lilly! My precious ones. What a surprise! This brings me tears of joy!"

She named eleven people but hugged fourteen, while my grandmother was bent over, submitting to the embraces of her sons and daughters-in-law and babbling, "Come in, come in. Is it really you? Come inside one at a time. I wish to see all of you up close before I die. Did everyone come? Welcome to this house, which is yours!"

Everybody was weeping and even I began to cry while my little brothers and sisters looked on, frightened by the onslaught. Our neighbors, seeing us in tears, began crying, too, without asking why.

My grandmother stationed herself by the door, and one by one she let them in, touching the faces of her sons and daughters-in-law whom she hadn't seen in fifteen years. Her sight was so weak that she pawed at them as if she were blind. Only her tears lent an air of life to her eyes, and I was afraid she would really die.

"Say hello to your aunts and uncles," my mother

said. By way of explanation, she added, "These are my brothers and their wives. Please, Boris, I beg you: put down your suitcase!"

Taking advantage of the confusion, my little brother opened a suitcase belonging to one of our uncles, emptied the contents all over the floor and attempted to close himself up inside.

Aunt Boriska, or it could have been someone else since so many names and faces were new to me, gave my little brother a withering glance and then lifted him like a kitten out of the suitcase, which filled up again with all the sundries.



"Why don't you sit, Mama?" my mother said to Grandma while she dried her eyes on the arm of one of her brothers.

My grandmother rebuffed my mother and kept running her hand over her children's faces while gleefully saying, "Marek, my little one. Are you always cheerful like you used to be, my baby boy?"

I burst out laughing. "He's probably forty years old," I said to my younger brothers and sisters. "They're all older than Papa but she can't see them so she calls them little."

"Hush, silly one!" my mother shouted.

All of a sudden everyone looked at us children at once, as if they'd only just noticed our presence. Mama had us go around to each person, insisting we kiss their hands.

Out front, a crowd of onlookers had gathered. Our closest friends wanted to come inside and chat, but Mama asked them to return later.

“I haven’t seen them in fifteen years,” she kept saying. “They all live abroad. I’d lost hope of ever seeing them . . .”

Mama could barely get from the kitchen to the bedroom; no one could move without stepping on someone else’s foot or stumbling over a suitcase.

My grandmother, who had finally sat down, was asking questions of pretty much everyone: “How are your children, David? And your oldest, Moshe, is he still sick? What about your rheumatism, Joseph? And you, Ivan? Hurry, tell me everything. What about your wife, Marek? Are you still arguing? That woman is a nuisance!”



“We have time, Mama,” Aunt Lilly interrupted. “We’re staying with you for all of Passover.”

“Oh heavens!” said my mother, who sent me over to our neighbors to ask for lodging. But she immediately called me back to her.

“You have to tell them to collect all the eggs the hens lay over the next few days. Ask for some potatoes, too,” she shouted. “Wait! Where are you running off to without money?”

My mother elbowed her way into the bedroom, climbed on a stool, and pulled a handkerchief tied with a knot from the back of the closet.

“What’s that, Mama?” I asked.

“Money. It was meant to pay for an operation, but Boris’s tonsils will have to wait. Go now! Run and pay right away for whatever they give you.”

I went to every house in town to ask for eggs and potatoes. I bought three kilos of sugar and fourteen new plates, five hens and a big, beautiful goose.

Anxious, my mother asked after I'd returned, "Did you find rooms?"

"Oh, I forgot," I said. "I was only thinking about food. Having the money to pay without haggling, I felt like a queen."

"You lost your head!" my mother yelled while she counted up the money. Thirty fillér was missing from the change. "And you lost money!"

We were in the privy. We'd holed up in there because she didn't want her brothers and sisters to see us and cover a share of the expenses.

"I bought some nuts. I'd been wanting them for so long. Don't scold me, Mama. I had the money and I couldn't resist."

"Where are they?"

"I ate them."

"It's fine. Everything's fine. But you have to help me find rooms for your aunts and uncles."

"Give me another thirty fillér," I said, taking advantage of the occasion.

"Take it," Mama said, "and try to convince the Szabos to give us the two nicest rooms, the biggest ones. Tell them your father will stop by and pay them somehow. Then go to the Fabians—they don't have children either. Ask for two more rooms. Tell them I'll send you there for a week to harvest potatoes because those people won't do anything for nothing."

When I came back, I told her Mr. Szabo had refused to rent me rooms with the excuse that he had a ferocious dog and if it bit one of the aunts or uncles, it would cost him a lot of money, and his dog can't be chained up because thieves would get wise immediately.

"Go to the Mallais," my mother said. "Run! Before it's nighttime."

Old Widow Mallai had three rooms and she lived by herself but she didn't want to hear my pleas.

"I'm poor," she said, "but I don't rent rooms to strangers. They're coming from afar, who knows what kinds of ways they might have. No, I can't do that."



"Go to the Nemeths," my mother said. "Offer the money right away because they're greedy."

When Mr. Nemeth heard eight uncles had arrived with their wives, he cleared his throat and gave a long speech about politics from which the only thing I understand was he didn't want to be around Jews.

We managed to have four of my uncles hosted by the Fabians. Like a threat, darkness was coming ever closer and my mother was truly desperate. We filled two sacks with straw so that the four of us children would sleep on the floor while the couch and the bed were left for Aunt Boriska, Aunt Lilly, Aunt Iren, Aunt Fanny, and Aunt Helen. To find the remaining spots, I went to five Jewish families who could not refuse to rent us rooms, even if they reluctantly agreed. My grandmother's bed was in the storage closet, which was separated from the kitchen by a partition made of colored paper. It was also the pantry. Grandma ate very little, and next to Mama, was the most trustworthy person in the family. She watched out so we children didn't wander in a hundred times a day to swipe some fruit preserves or stick our fingers in the honey. The pantry that smelled of mildew was her fiefdom.

Luckily, my father came home late for dinner. When he saw all of the people in the kitchen, he said, "Did Grandma die?"

Mama ran to him. "Karl, my brothers have come. All of them!"

The men hugged my father, and the women shook his hand. They were related but had only ever seen each other once, at my parents' wedding in Prague. Mama had come immediately to live here with my father, bringing along my grandmother who in no way wanted to be apart from her only little girl.

"You've gotten older, Karl," my Uncle David said.

"The years go by for all of us," said my father, glancing at his brother-in-law's healthy belly, "but I see you've had some very good years."

"It's your fault," said Aunt Iren. "You didn't want to move to Czechoslovakia. You forced Arina to live here, without making her happy."

My mother jumped up. "No one forced me. My place is with him. Please, Irenke, let's not start."

Before dinner, the aunts and uncles gave out gifts. My mother cried once more, pressing each item to her chest. They showered us children with candies, and we ran up and down the house in our rubber boots, which were so big Mama said we would put them aside until we'd grown. Grandma wanted to immediately put on her soft, wool dress, which was a gift from her daughters-in-law, and she placed in her pocket an envelope of money given to her by her sons. Even my father was touched; he got a wool jacket and he didn't look half bad.

"You look so nice!" all of us children shouted. "Put the scarf on, too. So handsome!"

Mama blushed from joy and she mustered the courage to say, "My Karl looks younger than everyone in his jacket."



My affection for my aunts and uncles began to grow and I buzzed around them, trying to make myself useful by performing small tasks that often earned me some pocket change. I'd never seen so much money in my life and I ran off to spend it on nuts with my girlfriends in town.

Papa was counting down the days that remained in the Passover holidays and spoke less and less. Sometimes I took him by surprise while he was confiding in my mother.

"Your brothers will eat us out of house and home in a single week," I heard him say.

"Don't worry, Karl, I have the money," she replied. "I'll take care of it."

"You're a good woman," he said, convinced the guests were covering a share of the expenses.

After that, even though he was worried about the money, he became more demanding each day about the food.

At the final meal, my father offered a toast: "Jews go to ruin at Passover, Muslims for weddings, and Christians in court!"

Everyone laughed, except my mother.

On the eighth day, my aunts and uncles left,

beaming. At the door, the same scene as when they arrived unfolded again. Grandma wanted to embrace her sons one by one and she praised them until they disappeared at the end of the road.

With great relief, we took back our own beds that night.

"What a family you have!" my father was shouting. "They cleaned out the house, they ate like pigs and what's more, they did nothing but criticize me while they lived in the lap of luxury for a week at my expense!"

"Some luxury!" my mother replied. "In fifteen years, you offered them eight days of hospitality."

"What did they ever offer me? Criticism. You could have told me earlier that I was paying for everything. You robbed me of the pleasure of stating that to them."

"Let me die in peace," my grandmother said, closing her eyes.

"Your mother is capable of dying out of spite."

The next day, Grandma did in fact die.

"She was waiting until after her sons had come and gone," Mama said, as she howled with grief.

They wrapped Grandma in a sheet and placed her on two planks without nails, in keeping with observant Jewish custom. Uncovered in that way, her soul would exit without difficulty. After the funeral, everyone sat on the straw laid on the floor as a sign of mourning. Mama was either praying or wailing. Only that evening did she realize Papa hadn't torn the collar of his jacket as a sign of grief.

"Your jacket, Karl," my mother said in a somber voice.

"I can't," Papa said. "It's new."

"Tear it," Mama said.

"I threw out the other jacket that was ripped and I cannot tear this one because it's new. Please, Arina, try to understand. It's important for business."

"You should get up," she said. "How are you in mourning if you don't tear your jacket?"

"I don't have other jackets," Papa said. "You always say God sees all. That He understands all. Well, He knows why I'm not tearing the collar on the new jacket. You can see it."

"I will mend it so you cannot even realize that it's been re-sewn," Mama said in tears.

"You must understand, Arina," my father said. "It's the first thing your family has given me in fifteen years, after your father disinherited me as an insult. I need this jacket and I won't tear it."

"Then get up!" my mother said. "If you remain sitting, you cannot leave your collar untorn."

"I'm making plenty of sacrifices for your mother," my father said. "I'm missing a week of work."

"Let him rest here at home with us, Mama," I said.

"Get up, Karl," my mother said.

"Really, how long it's been since I've rested," my father said. "You make me pine for the year I spent in prison in Trieste!"

Offended, my mother said, "We're not here to rest. You sit but you mustn't lean back. If you've decided not to tear your jacket and to lean back like a prince, then get up immediately and leave the house! If you don't, I'll leave and I won't ever come back."

My mother made as if to get up and my father went white as a sheet while an old tic took over his right cheek. Still seated, he grabbed the collar with his two hands and yanked it. He said nothing for a moment, staring at the long scrap of fabric that hung from his fingers.

"Blame it on the fabric," he said very quietly. "Isn't that right, Arina? My old beaten up one is better than the jacket from your brothers."

"Sit up straight," my mother said. "Don't lean against the wall. We're not resting, we're grieving. My mother has died. Say a prayer."

# *The Verdict*

"What did he say?" my mother shouted to me as I returned from the courtyard of the small synagogue where the shochet worked every Thursday.

It wasn't always the same person, but they all dressed in black wool tunics buttoned at the collar, which they wore even in the summer, and a stiff hat with a round brim that was also black. In the Jewish faith, he alone is authorized to slaughter the animals and to judge, for the observant, if meat may be consumed. Only he can utter the word "kosher," to indicate that the animal was healthy, and the word "trefa," which for all of us meant "forbidden."

Every Thursday, my mother worried about the shochet's verdict; if it was trefa, no one ate in our house, so inside this simple word hid a problem that needed resolving, and my mother had every reason to be impatient and worried and to shout, halfway between our house and the synagogue, "Answer me, would you?" But I'd never reply: if it was kosher, I'd walk forward with my head high, singing, and stroking the lifeless carcass of the animal I carried tucked under my arm—a chicken, goose, or duck, depending on how rich or poor we were at that moment. If it was trefa—and sometimes it was—I neared the house with my head hanging low, walking slowly, lacking the courage to tell my mother the truth. Sometimes I didn't go home right away but instead walked around with the dead goose, my head dangling like that of the animal bumping against my calf, often bloodying my leg and clothes. My mother would then blame me for everything—my thoughtless wandering, the animal that couldn't be consumed and the missing Sabbath dinner.



My mother was extremely good at divvying up the bird into even twenty portions, while we children whined about the piece of meat on our plates so thin it was transparent. We'd begin to argue, saying Margo got more than me and Peter more than Margo while Beni had a whole wing. She would stand there holding the pot, scooping out remnants from the bottom, which was never more than a leg or, at best, a piece of neck.

"Don't make me suffer," she was always saying. "Don't argue, it breaks my heart! You don't need to fill your bellies up with meat!" But we'd say that there was a big difference between filling up on meat and pretending to eat it, and at least once we'd like to see a whole cooked goose on our plate. Mama would reply, "And tomorrow what would I give you to eat? A lot of talk for a piece of meat. If there's a war, or an epidemic, or a hurricane, what would I feed you? Luckily you don't know what you're talking about. And all this on Shabbat!"

We often tried uselessly to convince my mother to serve the whole goose in one sitting; I believe her greatest skill lay in dividing up portions. There's a Thursday in every week, but it wasn't every Thursday that we had chicken or duck to bring to the shochet, and my friends would cast aspersions, asking why I hadn't gone to the synagogue yard that day. I said my mother had forgotten and that in our house we were all worrying over the fattened, month-old goose force-fed with corn that was so fat it might die before next Thursday.



"Bah!" they would say. "We want to believe what you're saying. Are you all just poor, or a bunch of liars, too?"

One Thursday, I arrived with a very nice duck and immediately afterwards, I swore I'd never set foot in the synagogue yard again. People were all lined up waiting for the shochet and the women murmured restlessly that a new one would be coming that day. Each of them had an animal wedged under her arm, maybe two or even as many as three, tied by their feet. Those who employed a Christian maid had her carry the animals but, not trusting the woman, came along to hear the verdict. Other women, all Christians, stood outside the synagogue, also waiting. I knew they were there to haggle over the rejected fowl that were deemed impure, offering scrawny chickens that couldn't have weighed more than half a kilo in exchange. When I walked by, they would say, "I hope it's trefa." They knew this word very well, and I would look at them angrily, once even saying to a pregnant woman who touched my duck, "I hope your child is born trefa!"

So between the line of Christian women praying for one result and the line of Jews praying for the opposite, I anxiously awaited my turn, and the person I hated most was the shochet.

He was a short, slight man with reddish hair and a sallow, freckled face who wore polished white eyeglasses on the end of his nose. He looked like a god come down to earth, strict and uncourteous. With a professional air, he ordered that the animals be tied up well and insisted that everyone bring along a mound of ashes to collect the blood. The ritual was the same: holding the animal by the legs, he would jerk the head back and make a single cut under the throat, then throw it on the pile with the others, leaving it there to writhe. It was a horrific sight and it was repeated every Thursday. He would twist the victim's wings with impressive speed and then pluck feathers from the neck that flew onto his face and ours while he blew them away. With a wide, sharp knife, he made the final cut, letting the blood flow onto the mound of ashes. But only for a moment, because if the animal bled too much, he would call the owner over to help by putting a foot on its head and pulling it by the legs to drain the blood. Then, hovering between life and death, the wretched goose or chicken was added to the pile in the corner, beating its wings wildly, to the right and to the left, fueled by the scant blood that remained. The shochet's right hand was bloody, and sweat pooled on his face and behind his glasses, now stained red, but he showed no sign of nausea or fatigue. He just repeated, with a sharp but low voice, "Next! Step forward!" The animals, meanwhile, would flutter around the yard in their last, low flight.

I stood there in a light summer dress and every so often, I felt something hot drip on my face and I hated all of mankind.

When he was done with the last animal, he paused at the entrance to the synagogue, lifting his face toward us for the first time. Each woman began looking through the pile for her chicken, her duck, her goose, recognized by an identifying mark on the feet: ribbons and bows in every color.

The animals whose throats had been slit first were already dead, and their owners pulled them from the pile and waited respectfully.

"One at a time, in order," the arbiter thundered. Holding up a chicken, he said, "Whose is this?"

A poor man came forward—that was clear from the scrawniness of the meager chicken, and also, judging by his eyes, his anxiety about the shochet's verdict. The shochet poked two white fingers inside the wound he'd made, rummaged around, and removed the esophagus, bringing it to his soft, moist lips. Then he blew inside, holding the two ends tightly so no air escaped. It was like a bladder, a taut, transparent balloon that the judge held up before his eyes, inspecting every millimeter. A quick examination meant it was kosher and we would all guess as much right away, even before he announced it. But if the judge had any doubts, and carefully stretched a finger so as not to let the air escape and began to scratch its little, barely visible black spots, it would be forbidden. In the course of a few minutes, he blew five or six times, announcing, "Yes, no, trefa, kosher," and faces lit up or darkened as people left the yard and headed home or lingered outside to barter with the Christians, not seeking a good price or arguing over weight, but instead accepting little in exchange, since as good observant Jews, they couldn't cook an animal that wasn't kosher.



One day, my father returned home with a goose that was to be fattened in three weeks. But my mother didn't appear satisfied and she got enough grain for five weeks so that the goose would reach eight kilos.

"I'll show you," she shouted, "my goose will be the fattest in the whole village! No more gossip or mean looks; my daughter won't have to be ashamed anymore of the skinny little chickens we feed her so often. They'll see the kind of goose my family eats. It will be Fat Thursday!"

She then ordered me to clean the closet where the goose would be left to squawk for five weeks. I put down fresh straw, changed its water, and twice a day—once in the morning, and again at night—I stroked the beautiful feathers while carrying the animal from its little home into the kitchen. There, the salted grain was ready, along with a drop of oil to help the food go down. Straining, we placed the goose between my mother's fleshy thighs because the poor beast was moaning and resisting with the force of a man. Mama opened the goose's beak with great effort, fed it handfuls of corn and massaged it to ease the mash down to the stomach. But more often than not, the animal spit it all back up.

"This one is a bear," my mother would say. "It won't ever get fat. It doesn't want to and it resists too much. I think I'll be the one who dies first, from the effort."





After a couple of weeks, the goose seemed resigned to this torture, like a man who gets beaten so often he stops feeling the pain, thinking of nothing but the end. The goose, which was meant to become the pride of the family, had grown docile, but wasn't gaining weight like we wanted. Its feathers were wretched and it waddled slowly, heavily, and at night it moaned all alone; no one could sleep hearing its cries.

"I'm going to strangle it before it's ready," my father fumed. "Is it possible that a stupid beast could ruin my life all day and all night?"

Then he turned to my mother, and said, "You do nothing but say, 'I wonder if it's digested. Can someone check if it has water? Why is it crying? And now why isn't it making any noise? Why this, why that?' It's become the center of attention! If I ask for a glass of water, which one of you goes running? But if it's for the goose, then everyone runs and why? Your stomachs! You have no other goal in life, you think of nothing else . . . either you kill it next Thursday or I'm going to kill it myself with my bare hands, you got it?"

"When are you ever home?" my mother replied defensively. "Even your children bother you now, you can't stand anyone and you take it out on the goose. But you want to eat, don't you? Your children make you nervous and yet they didn't make you nervous when you were making them . . . only now that you have to raise them, take care of them, play with them!"

Their argument had gone well beyond the goose and I tried to interrupt even though I knew later they would be angry with me and my "rotten philosophy." "Why did you bring me into this world?" I said. "Surely not for my own pleasure. Now there are too many of us and you have trouble feeding us. It's not like I feel all that happy to be alive . . ."

My words always met the same end every time, which was hearing them ask where I came from and who'd taught me such things. "One knows these things," I would reply. "One reads. I see nothing but suffering and poverty all around me. If everyone is crying, there must be a reason: sickness, hunger, money, war . . . these are the riches of the chosen people!"

"You're the scourge of the family," my mother would shout. "You take God's name in vain!"

"It's not true," I replied angrily. "I don't speak to God or King Solomon, and besides they wouldn't answer me. I'm talking to all of you and none of you understand me. You know how to talk but not how to truly laugh or rejoice." I started shouting. "And you, Mama! When have I ever seen you laugh? I, who live with you and am your daughter: when have you ever had joy to share with me? How can I believe in your happiness if I've never seen you smile? As for you, Papa, you shove it all down like this goose eating animal feed, you swallow and swallow without ever digesting anything. What do you expect out of life? No, don't cry, Mama, I wish I could see you happy."

At this point, I was crying, too, and the truth stood between us like a giant wall that leaves no room for joy among people who love each other.



I carried on taking the goose back and forth for the usual torture. One day, a piece of food went down the wrong way, got stuck and wouldn't move up or down, causing the animal to choke. Mama shook it while shouting, "What should we do? My God, if it dies on me now! Run to Julka's house now. Quick!"

I grabbed the goose, which was barely breathing, and I hurried over to the house belonging to the woman who cured animals and children with cooked onion, spider webs and milk, and some herbs she herself prepared and administered. This was why the whole town admired her; she was called a wizard, a saint, blessed by God if it worked. If it didn't, she was a witch or a damn quack!

My mother ran right behind me, still shouting, "Hurry! It's dying! Or is it still alive? See if it's warm."

By now, the goose was meekly moaning while my mother slowed down, still shouting to me from the street to hurry up and not be waylaid by chit-chat.

Julka wasn't home, she had been called out for an urgent birth, and her old mother said her daughter didn't treat animals anymore, not in a village where the doctor only visits a few months out of the year.

"He's always away," she added, "and when he gets here, all he finds is dead bodies. He's here for show—he's not like my daughter who has become a known healer." The old woman kept talking but I couldn't hear on account of the goose's cold body. I glanced at the bird. It felt heavier now that it was dead and I positioned the head between the wings to keep the green liquid from dripping out of its slack beak. I ran outside and asked a peasant woman I knew if she had a knife, urging her to go quick since the goose was dying.

"Oh good," she said. "Will you sell it to me? It's not kosher so you might as well."

"Hurry up," I yelled. "It's dying!"

She handed me a knife and said, "Are you going to kill it? If your God won't allow you, let me throw on a shawl and I'll do it."

By the time she returned, I had already made three or four incisions in the neck, cutting in a zig zag out of nervousness, but the blood didn't flow out and instead trickled out drop by drop.

She looked at me and the goose with the same contempt.

"It's already a bit of a carcass," she said, "even if you think it's fine for us. It's not good enough for any of you, isn't that right, Little Miss Fussy?"

While I was arguing with the woman to trade for a skinnier goose that was still alive, my mother arrived.

"Your daughter wants to sell me a slaughtered beast that's already dead. Otherwise, she wouldn't have asked for a knife and without waiting for me sliced its throat to bits."

My mother was startled. "You? Did you kill it yourself? Answer me!"

"Only half-way," I murmured quickly. "It was already mostly dead . . ."

"If you like," the woman said, "I'll give you five hatching eggs for it."

"No," I replied. "Give me a chicken we can eat right away."

Mama stared silently at the goose that lay between the woman and me.

"Well," the woman said after a brief pause, "my man likes liver the way you Jews prepare it and this goose must have a big fat one, so all right."

We gathered all of her animals into the yard with some grain, and we each grabbed one, even though the woman berated me, saying, "Put back that one."

"If only I had so many animals," my mother sighed.

"But you people have money even under your skin!" the woman replied.

"Which one will you give me?" I said. "I want the one I'm holding."

"You have a good eye, eh?" she said. "You people know everything, but today is Sunday and I don't want to wear myself out arguing. I'll have too much to do handling this goose you've fattened up so nicely." She weighed it in her hands, adding, "It's like a little piglet!"

"Since you have so many animals, why don't you do what we do?" I said.

"We raise them to buy fabric and tablecloths and many other necessary things that we don't have, while you people . . ."

"How do you know," I interrupted her, ready to argue, "that we have all of these things?"

"What Jew doesn't?" she said. "Besides, you manage among yourselves—you're all connected, unlike us."

I wanted to say more but my mother yanked me by the dress so that I would quit talking once and for all.

While we were walking away, I said, "How stingy these farmers are, and they think we Jews all take care of each other."

"And why would you want to prove the opposite?" my mother asked.

I walked, my eye on my mother, and I'd have liked to explain to her that we're all the same, that there are rich people and poor people all over, and that it's good to know each other's flaws so that we don't become isolated. But instead, I said only, "What do you expect her to know about what's cooking in our pot?"

By now, we'd arrived back home and all of my brothers and sisters were outside. As soon as they saw us with the chicken, they understood the situation. By the set of their mouths, it was clear they were about to burst into tears.

Glancing at my mother, my father said, "Deborah dear, I think your God pays little attention to all your prayers."

"It's your fault," Mama replied, "because I have to pray for you, for the children, for health and for peace in the family, and it leaves me little time for small matters. That's why the goose is dead! And I now have to ask forgiveness for your daughter's sacrilege after she slaughtered a beast that was already dead and managed to exchange it for this chicken."

"What are you going to do? Sometimes necessity trumps the law."

I was there but I said nothing, satisfied simply to watch my father as he added, "I got some work. I'll transport grain to the city using a friend's wagon. Maybe they won't pay me only in money. I'll ask for food as compensation and I'll bring everyone a duck if I can manage it. I'll have to make three trips, all at night, because my friend needs the wagon during the day to work the fields."



Hearing about the prospect of work, my mother calmed down and, approaching my father, said, "Wear a coat and may God be with you."

There were other lean Thursdays and fat Thursdays, and despite my pledge, I wasn't able to avoid visiting the synagogue yard, since I was the strongest in the house, and able to hold the animal still while it twisted in my arms, under the shadow of death. And, every time, I couldn't keep myself from hating the shochet and waiting anxiously for the holy word that for us meant eating or not eating. In that Jewish word which the judge pronounced coldly and quickly, the plight of so many families was concealed. There were more lean Sabbaths, as we called them, than fat ones, and more often than not, we ate beans and toast or not even beans. And every Thursday, my mother met me halfway between our house and the synagogue, with her apron rolled up around her waist. That was her way of being elegant and stepping out into the street when she was too rushed to take time to remove it.

Mama, today I'd tell you a big fat lie, because the world's hunger is bigger than your religion—I would shout from the street that it's always kosher! So many blades grazed our hearts, so many small cuts made them bleed, and they weren't in a zig-zag like mine. Other surer, colder hands have operated on live men and not on a dead goose.

# *At the Foot of the Bed*

"Whose turn is it tonight?"

My mother's voice left an embarrassed silence over the table. We'd just finished scarfing down the last bite of our meager dinner, and we stared at each other for a while before venturing a response.

"Not me," I was the first to say, straightening up in the chair to seem taller and give more heft to my words.

"Actually, it is your turn, shorty," said my brother, Árpád, to make me angry.

"Let's figure it out," I said. "The last time was the night with the creamed potatoes. I remember it well—I still have the taste in my mouth. And don't call me shorty, got it?"

"That was Tuesday," my mother calmly stepped in. "Today is Thursday so it's truly your turn, Aniko."

"That's good to hear because when it's Aniko's turn, I sleep better," Papa said, turning to me. "You're the only one who knows how to massage my back right."

"And you'll give my feet a little massage," my mother said, to the merriment of my brothers.

The idea of sleeping once again at the foot of the big bed didn't thrill me at all so I looked imploringly at Tibor, who was the oldest of all of us and made some money working as an errand boy at a tailor's shop. To console me, he said, "I'll give you twenty *filler* if you give my shoes a proper polish before going to school tomorrow morning. You have to wipe them with a damp cloth and smooth them out like new, otherwise I won't pay you."



"I'm not going to sleep at the foot of the big bed," I replied, "and I won't polish your busted shoes, not even for a pengő because . . . I'm tired."

Everyone burst into laughter. Papa promised me a tennis ball that I'd been wanting since seeing my cousin play in the freshly-mowed fields with a friend who was better off.

"Don't give anything to her, Pop-Pop, because today's really her turn," Árpád said. "If you promised to give us each a gift for sleeping at the end of the bed, it would cost less to just buy a new bed."

"For now, promises don't cost anything," my father said.

My mother, who saw anything new as the enemy, said she had no intention of converting the house into a dormitory. What was all this talk? Her children had always slept like that until they were twelve, when—having finished school—they left home one by one to find work in the city: the first child, the second, the third, the fourth, all well-mannered children who insisted on very little. Now though, for two snot-nosed boys and one little snot-nosed girl, family traditions should be changed? All because Tibor doesn't want to leave their town. Árpád isn't keen on working at home or in the city, and Aniko, who hasn't even finished school, is full of demands!



My father felt he had to intervene. "We won't argue over such a silly thing," he said, looking at us children. "At your age, I was happy to sleep at the foot of my parents' bed. In winter back then, I wouldn't give up that spot to anyone. Of course, it didn't leave me much room to grow."

Amused, he got up from his chair and stood next to Mama, gently steering her against the wall. He wanted us children to be the judges. He wasn't a giant, and seeing him next to Mama, he looked just like a pigmy.

"I don't want to be a half-pint forever," I said and began to laugh. "I am already so short that everyone at school makes fun of me. Now I understand why I can't grow!"

Mama became testy. "What ideas are you putting in this girl's head? You always joke at the worst possible time. You know all too well Aniko gives us a hard time when it's her turn, thrashing and whining like an actress!"

I looked at my mother; maybe it was a good time to suggest something I'd been mulling over since dinner began.

"I'd like to at least move my turn so instead of Tuesday and Thursday, I'd prefer two days in a row, maybe Friday and Saturday," I said in one quick go.

"Oh, that's a good one! And why is that?" came a chorus of replies.

"That way I won't have to think about it at the beginning of the week. If you let me have those two nights, I won't complain about anything else."

"Well to begin with, Friday is my day," Árpád said, "and also, it's your turn not twice a week but three times, just like me. Tibor is the one who's able to only sleep one night in Mama and Papa's bed because he's grown, he works and we can't expect him not to sleep well . . ."

My mother interrupted him. "Since when haven't you slept well in the big bed?"

"Oh, I'm just saying Tibor is a working man . . ." Árpád replied, embarrassed.

"If he works and makes money, why doesn't he buy a bed all for himself?" I said, jumping up. "Someone who works can buy what he wants. You'll see when I'm working!"

"Right, like having a job brings in enough to live decently," my father said, with a half-smile. "When you get bigger, you'll understand it's not how you imagine it'll be when you're eight, or however old you are."

Stunned, mother replied, "Don't you know your daughter's age?"

"I don't even know my own age," my father said. "Age is something I feel in my body—I don't count years like you women do. But in this house, as soon as you open your mouth, every joke becomes a big deal. If one says 'glass of water,' in the course of talking, it becomes the sea. If instead one talks about the sea, he's scolded for dreaming because in this house there isn't a well where you can draw water. And that's just an example . . ."

With these comments, Papa had, as usual, set himself on a collision course and now that he'd started, he wasn't even looking for our approval but instead turned directly to Mama.



"Can you tell me, Deborah, why a poor man works?"

"Because he has no choice," my mother responded, calmly. "Or did I have these seven children by myself?"

Tibor elbowed Árpád who had covered his face with his hands to hide that he was laughing. But I found it to be a very serious matter and I said, "You grownups don't even know who brought your children into the world but you're quick to shove them to the foot of the bed where there's no room for them to grow!"

My mother had tears in her eyes; for a moment, I feared she was crying and I was already regretting what I'd said, even if I didn't remember exactly the words that could have offended her. Then I saw her belly was shaking out of immense laughter and I realized everyone would give their two cents that night without arguing.

"So, you want Friday and Saturday and maybe even Sunday? And why is that, shorty?" my brother said, continuing to prod me.

"Because I like those days," I said.

Árpád persisted. "There's another reason, isn't there?"

"It's none of your business," I said curtly.

Now even the big people were curious to know why I'd specifically chosen those days of the week. I finally worked up my nerve and I said, "Because on Friday we all give ourselves a good washing."

My brothers understood immediately and looked over at me, their eyes full of gratitude. I was the youngest but I'd had the courage to complain about my father's habit of getting in bed dirty and sweaty after a whole day out in the fields or in the dirty streets of our Zemplén region.



Indignant, my father protested: "In my family, I always took care of my body."

"I can only imagine the rest of them," I said, without any malice. I could feel my brothers' growing admiration for my courage.

"If you want your father to get washed every night," said my mother, who had taken my comment badly, "all you need to do is heat up some water. I've been sleeping with him for twenty years and I can't say anything against his feet, which are small and slender. And small feet don't sweat."

My father fell into a grumpy silence. I approached him with a kiss in an effort to win him back, but my mother was more convincing.

"It's not like she took the crown from your head," she said. "Are you not a man who for work must walk from morning until night? Your shoes are often in bad shape and sometimes they even get muddy, right?"

"My children are mocking me," my father said in the most serious tone yet.

He seemed truly offended and began to complain that he couldn't wear different shoes every day, and that he couldn't get the pair of shoes he had resoled because he'd lose a day of work, and that in our house we couldn't waste water because it took a lot of effort to draw it from the well, and of his spoiled children whom he had to beg on bended knee to get them to fill two buckets.

"You're all afraid of dogs," he went on, his fervor growing, "and afraid of the dark or if it's broad daylight, of the insane or of anti-Semites. You all have an excuse for saying no and you squeal like a monkey: 'I'm not going!' 'Why don't you ask Tibor?' And Tibor says, 'Why don't you send Aniko?' You don't obey me. One day, all of you will understand that it's not always easy to get cleaned up in life."

"All right, that's enough," Mama said sympathetically. "Don't spoil the evening over a pair of feet that your daughter doesn't like. Shall we all wish her the best in finding a man with nicely-scented feet? No, Aniko?"

I felt very guilty, but I didn't want to admit it. So I said, "I won't care at all about my husband's feet. If he gives me a bed all for myself, I won't ask for anything else."

"Oh forget the idea that he's going to give you a bed for yourself," my youngest brother, Árpád, cried out.

"Well then I won't get married," I replied.

"Can we get quit talking about beds and feet?" my father said sadly.

He began taking off his waistcoat and preparing for the night. Then he sat down on the big bed and said in a voice that was both sweet and serious, "How lucky you are to sleep at our feet. Where else will you find such a warm, snug spot?"

# *Reading French Poetry After the War*

IMMEDIATELY AFTER the war, when you could still read the signs of hunger on our faces, orphan girls like us had more parents than friends. Everyone—relatives distant or close—wanted to be our parents. If it was a man, he would say, "Listen, I could be your father. You know that I'm speaking for your own good." If it was a woman, she already felt like she was our mother and she didn't stint on advice.

At that time, I was living with an aunt who had been a model old maid until she was forty, managing even to survive the tragedy of our people. But once liberation arrived, feeling more alone than ever, she desperately set about looking for a husband. She ended up finding a man in his fifties, a recent widower, big as an ox and cheerful as a lark; at home, if he wasn't singing, he whistled the melodies of the many songs he knew. This aunt and my new uncle served as my parents for a few months back in 1945.

I had to take care of everything, even lunch and dinner, because before the war, my aunt, who didn't know how to cook, had inherited a small shop from her father that reopened when she married. "A customer!" she would announce joyfully when she heard the door bell, running down the stairs as she fixed her mane of red hair, which was always in disarray. I don't know how she managed not to trip as she ran toward the door that led from the house to the store, searching her pockets for her eyeglasses, which were for nearsightedness. Then she stopped in front of the mirror and dabbed a wad of cotton into a heavy white flour-like powder mixture that even in those days could barely pass for face powder. She smoothed it on her skin to hide the freckles that covered her face, finally ready to receive and serve customers. I waited for those moments because if my aunt made any sales, she was more amenable to me.

Then I would say, "I'd like to go out. I have to see Eva."

"Eva?" she replied, astonished. Adopting a disapproving tone immediately, she said, "What fine friends you have."

"There's not a single book in this house," I would say. "I'd like to be able to read sometimes."

"That girl," my aunt would interrupt me, shouting, "is a brazen little number who got into the head of Rabbi Moskovitsch's son. I forget—you're not from here and don't know what a wonderful man he was and how he raised his sons! Two golden boys: one studies the Talmud and the other buys and sells wheat profitably. Two principled boys distracted by that hussy. If he were still alive, their poor father would die of shame. And as for me, since I could be your mother—in fact, I am like a mother to you! No, I won't let you choose the path of ruin."



My uncle was whistling outside the house, but, hearing his wife yell, he took his chubby hands out of his pockets and bravely came inside.

"What's the matter?" my uncle said. "Why are you angry, my fairy princess?"

"You just can't teach girls manners these days," my aunt said. "They aren't the way I was, they're on the wrong path. They know it and they're going to follow it all the way to the end."

"You were waiting for me, honey, weren't you?"

My uncle stepped closer to my aunt, and she immediately calmed down, tamed by the voice of her cheerful, melodic lark.

"Don't worry," my uncle went on, "every age has its thrills. Ours are more mature, right, sweetheart?"

He looked at his wife pointedly. "How much did you take in today?"

"A decent amount," she replied.

"Then why don't we close up and rest a bit?"

"Go ahead," they said as one, "but come back soon."

Behind my aunt's back, my uncle winked at me as he steered her gently toward the bedroom.

I found Eva waiting for me by the window. From her irritated look, I knew she had been punished by her "parents," a cousin and her husband, whom she'd lived with since the war.

"What did you do wrong?" I asked her quietly from the street because I dared not go inside the house.

"I burnt a shirt with the iron," Eva said. "I'd been ironing all afternoon and the coal had given me a headache. But they say I'm not thinking straight for other reasons—that I'm always in a hurry to leave so I can run over to Armin's house. And that's why I can't go anywhere. Go to him, please. He's waiting for me at the barn. Tell him I can't leave the house."

"Don't worry," I said, "I'll go. But I'd like that book—that's why I came."

"Not so loud," Eva said. "If they hear talk of a book in this house that's not a prayer book, it's like the end of the world. I'll give it to you tomorrow, Armin is reading it now. But don't say anything about the book—he'd be embarrassed with you. He can only talk about everything with me."

Eva assumed the air of a worldly woman to make people forget she was only sixteen and so that I would feel more keenly that I wasn't as old yet. I didn't even say goodbye in my haste to relay the message.

"The person you're waiting for," I said to Armin as soon as I arrived, "cannot leave the house because she is stuck there."

We weren't in the barn but rather in the large room on the ground floor that served as kitchen and dining room. The younger son of the late Rabbi Moskovitsch stammered in reply that he wasn't waiting for anyone. He was an attractive young man with overly pale skin that reminded me of someone who'd spent his whole life in prison without ever seeing the sun. He was embarrassed; he seemed as though he feared contact with the outside world, walking back and forth in the room as if in a cage. Stammering some more, he asked if I wanted to sit. Then his eyes searched desperately all around—for what, I don't know, because there were two chairs right there in front of him. He ran out of the room and when he returned, I was seated and forcing myself to talk with the older brother who stood motionless in the darkest corner, wearing a hat and dressed entirely for winter, in August. I had looked around and, seeing no woman in the home, ventured the question: "Who cooks for you?"

Before answering, the older brother vigorously scratched at the many blemishes covering his face.

"Mrs. Kleinmann," he said after a pause so long I felt an irrepressible desire to leave.

Armin returned without a chair, but when he saw I was already sitting, he heaved a sigh of relief as if he'd solved a huge problem and settled himself as far away as possible. Addressing me formally, he said, "How are you?"

He moved around in his seat uncomfortably, like a baby bird in a new nest.

"Good," I said. "I just started living with my aunt, whom you know better than I do."

"We used to see her sometimes before the war," Armin said, "when our parents were still alive. Our father often gave advice to your aunt's grandfather who couldn't find a husband for her. Almost every Saturday, our families talked over a new possibility. Mind you, they weren't the richest or most attractive men in town. Once, our father introduced a cousin who was a small, skinny man who fully intended to marry her. We were still children, but I remember our families no longer spoke after your aunt refused. That's why I was embarrassed when I saw you a moment ago."

From his corner, the older brother reproached him with his eyes for telling that old story.

"I heard Mr. Kleinmann's new wife is a relative of yours," I said.

"She was Rabbi Reisman's wife. A third cousin of my father's."

The older brother remained silent.

"The new Mrs. Kleinmann is very young and beautiful," I said. "Mr. Kleinmann didn't stay a widower for long, either."

"Everyone marries quickly now," said Armin, twisting his pale hands. "No one wants to be alone."

Annoyed, the older brother stood up, walked by me, and left without saying goodbye. I immediately capitalized on this.

"Eva's been punished," I said under my breath. "Poor thing, she couldn't come at all."

Armin didn't answer. A moment later, he, too, got up and told me to give his regards to my aunt, without saying goodbye to me.

When I arrived back home, my aunt was brooding as she wiped the furniture using a rag doused in oil and kerosene; the rooms had been invaded by an unpleasant odor and the few dark, heavy pieces of furniture glinted with sadness. My aunt's face was even redder than usual, and the tufts of curly hair that had been singed by the iron spilled out over her eyes from under the kerchief tied around her head. She went on the attack immediately: "This furniture is the only memento the war has left me untouched—you should take better care of it. But you young people aren't attached to anything . . ."



It was clear she hadn't rested well and her discontent made her even uglier; I couldn't say who she resembled as she was the lone redhead in the family. I lay down and watched her. She was scrubbing with exaggerated movements, her back to me, but it was as if she could see me.

"Don't put your feet up! Look at the sad state of this broken-down couch."

For the first time, I looked at the couch upholstered in very worn, frayed burgundy velvet; the springs no longer held, and I sank into a crevasse every time I moved.

I thought to myself, "How can I sleep here, with the dusty odors that come from inside, on this poorly stuffed straw mat?"

My aunt turned around and looked at me sideways. "You can't say I make you do too much around the house."

"You're talking too much," said a voice coming from the shop, surprising me with its harsh tone. It was the same voice that trilled from morning till night.

My aunt suddenly straightened up and, in a formal tone, said, "Sir, I can't allow you to speak to me in such a vulgar and offensive way."

"Quit crushing this girl's spirit."

My uncle entered the room and sat next to me on the couch, giving me a kiss for the first time.

With her elbow, my aunt brushed away the locks of hair that fell over her face, looked at us in astonishment, and suddenly went pale. I stood up and asked with genuine worry what was wrong; I had never seen her go pale before.



"Nothing," she said in an anguished voice, and burst into tears.

"My little turtledove, why are you crying?" my uncle said.

He tried to hug her, handing her a handkerchief, but my aunt roared angrily, "Don't touch me!"

"Can I help you?" I asked my aunt. I wanted to make peace. Her response—"Noooo!"—sent me running out of the house. When I returned, the silence was so deafening I tiptoed in and slid into bed without dinner.

The next day was a Saturday, our day off. Without saying anything at home, I went to Eva's house.

"Do you have the book?" I asked.

She handed me a package wrapped in a sheet of newspaper.

"Here it is," she said in a low voice. Then so that her cousin would overhear, she thanked me for lending her the book on the history of Zionism. Dumbfounded, I gave her a long stare before finally admiring her quick thinking. We said goodbye, agreeing to meet later for a swim at the river.

The road just beyond the village sloped gently upward, with a glimpse of the hilltop coming into view. The sun was lovely and mild, and boys and girls were playing around in the water or stretched out on the nearest bank. I saw a couple lying in the sun, wrapped in an embrace: a brother and sister I knew a little because they were my neighbors. At first, I thought, "Finally, two people who love each other." I sat down some distance away and waved at them. Lifting her head from her brother's lap, the girl looked at me for a moment, then she settled back into her position even more snugly than before, and in a short while, they began whispering and kissing each other. I thought about when my aunt and uncle were together and would be very loving, going off to rest together, and the thought frightened me. Embarrassed, I moved away from the brother and sister and went to sit at the water's edge, my bare feet in the water. I opened the package; finally, I had the book I'd long wished for—François Villon's poetry. I stared ahead at the dirty, yellow river. The far bank lay before me, the countryside full of fruit trees and semi-hidden farmers' cottages. Children dressed in rags spied on the bathers, snickering over our bathing suits and pointing. Slowly, a group of people drawn by our bare shoulders and legs gathered. The old women were shrieking to call the children back home and spitting on the ground. I instinctively covered myself with the newspaper. Unfolding the pages, I was drawn to a headline that took up half a page.

"Brothers," it read, "come back home!" Beneath it, in smaller letters, a line read, "Freedom calls! The homeland needs you as you need the homeland." It was a Zionist newspaper from Budapest. I read the article quickly, and suddenly I felt important; I was filled with a new, unexplainable joy. I had to talk to someone but Eva was late. At last, I saw her as she was crossing the field and I ran to her. Luckily, she was alone and I could speak freely. I asked her if she wanted to come to Israel with me. Right away, as I had already decided. By way of reply, she hugged me. She was trembling; finally, she said, something amazing had happened.



"Tell me quickly, there's no time to lose. I'm leaving."

"He kissed me!" she cried, through tears and laughter. "He kissed me."

"Who?" I asked. "Where and why?"

I remembered my uncle's kiss, which had provoked tension at home.

"Armin," she said after a pause. "He read the book of Villon's poetry and thought for two days and two nights about kissing me to show he's a man like Villon and can kiss like a poet—like Villon and his woman."

Eva looked at me, her eyes sparkling.

"So you'll marry now, you love each other," I said. "Why don't you both come with me to Israel?"

"I'll talk to Armin—he's fed up with his older brother who's always scolding him. He was just saying today that you can't live here like before; people have been poisoned by propaganda against Jews and we Jews are always convinced that they don't care for us. Armin says there's always an accusation in our eyes."

"Armin is smart," I said, "and we need a smart man who knows how to explain why we can no longer live in our own country."





I still had the book under my arm and I held the newspaper open to the page with the headline that seemed to fix my life. I was in a good mood, and returning home to my aunt and uncle, I knew I could count on this escape route. Peace had been restored, although I noticed my aunt was nervous in my presence. She didn't say anything, but at dinner she asked what was in the package.

"A book about Zionism," I said. "I'd like to read and understand what it is and then maybe—"

"Maybe what?" came their reply. "What do you need to understand at your age? Let's see the book."

"I can't, it's not mine. And besides . . . it's written for young people."

My uncle burst into melodious laughter. "I'm equal to three young people. Isn't that true, sweetheart? And if you don't believe me, child, I can show you—"

"You're such an idiot," my aunt said. "As if a pretty, young girl is interested in a man like you!"

"The young girls didn't turn me away before I married you," he said.

My uncle smiled with his mouth crooked, as though something pained him. Then he boisterously embraced his wife, asking that she testify to his romantic prowess.

"Don't speak that way in front of the child," she said. "I forbid it! Your coarseness knows no limits."

"You know you like it!" he shot back, laughing.

"God forgive me," she murmured to herself, "he has lost his mind."

They made up after my aunt's prayer and my uncle went back to whistling around the house, his hands in his pockets.

As soon as I was in bed, I began reading Villon's poems. I had dreamed as a child of going to Paris and now that I was reading his poetry, it seemed as though I knew the places where Villon had loved and hated. His women had been kissed like Eva, I noticed enviously, but there was no way Armin could kiss like Villon. I compared his Margo with Eva and concluded Armin would never have the courage to love a woman like Margo.

His poetry became for me a prayer that I repeated hundreds of times, I loved him and his Paris and his River Seine, and I rejected everything he rejected.

In the daytime, I hid Villon's poetry in the unlit stove, while my aunt grumbled about the book that I had brought home, which would surely ruin my character and my reputation.

"An obscene book," she would say. "The work of the Devil. No doubt it was your friend Eva who gave it to you, that shameless hussy."

"Why do you say that?" I replied angrily. "She's a nice girl."

"I know because of her cousin who is raising her. She told me Eva thinks of nothing but boys and leaves the house every chance she gets. She is ruining Rabbi Moskovitsch's son, people know about it and the whole town is talking. If his father were alive, Armin would never have looked at that girl."

"You're being unfair," I said. "Eva and Armin love each other, maybe even more than you and Uncle."

"You don't know what you're saying. At sixteen, no one is in love."



"I like it better when young people are in love. At least it looks good," I yelled, tearfully. Then I ran and threw myself on my bed.

One morning, I found my aunt beside my bed with curlers in her hair. *She looks like a scarecrow with the ties on those rollers*, I thought to myself. She was sitting by the window with her eyeglasses perched on her nose reading something. Widening my eyes, I saw it was my Villon book.

"My book!" I shouted. "Why did you take it? It's mine."

She didn't bother responding. She didn't lift her eyes. I was afraid because there were curses and also words that would make a Hungarian farmer blush, and I am sure in French it amounts to the same thing. I feared my aunt's reaction—and justifiably.

"Get up," she said, enraged. "We're going to Eva's house."

She was running, with the rollers on her head and her night shirt creeping out from her half-open robe. With one arm, she dragged me through the streets of our town barefoot and in pajamas, and with the other arm, she waved the book whose pages were flying away too quickly for me to collect.

"I gave you everything," my aunt was yelling. "You never went without, I was a mother to you! In my house, we don't read such filth. Ours is an honorable family!"

People were stopping to look and they laughed as I sobbed.



We got to Eva's house with the tattered book looking like a battle flag. Now my aunt was screaming even louder, with insults and explanations flying back and forth between the two sides. Armin was sent for; he glanced with embarrassment at me and my aunt looking the way we did, and then courageously said the book was his.

"Oh Lord!" both sides said in unison. "His father abandoned him, his soul has gone dark."

"They love each other," my aunt threw in. "Eva and Armin are in love."

"What? Get married immediately," said Eva's cousin. "My God, what a disgrace. What have you two done?"

Armin was confused—he couldn't grasp why there was a scandal nor was he able to calm down Eva's cousin, a strict thirty-something authoritarian woman.

Finally, he stammered, "How can I get married? I haven't done anything. How will I support a family?"

"After what's happened, you have to marry this poor girl who might be pregnant," my aunt said.

Eva became red as a beet, and looked at Armin who was even paler than usual, furious that he wasn't able to defend himself or her, and then she turned on all of us.

"I'm leaving. I'm going to Israel. I am fed up with everything and all of you. I want to be free. Here no one needs me—not the town, not any of you, not him," she said, pointing to Armin. "I can still have everything. There's room for young people there. I read it in the newspaper."



"I'm going with Eva," I said. "And you'll come with us, too, Armin, if you're a man."

"You've gone crazy," my aunt and Eva's cousin said, frightened. "How will you get there? Where will you get the money for the trip?"

"There's an organization in Budapest. They take care of everything—I read that, too." Eva was speaking calmly now. "Don't worry about the money."

Our two "mothers" heaved a sigh of relief and said that yes perhaps we could discuss it and consider the trip because, after all, for young people it could be a worthwhile project . . .

My aunt looked at me almost tenderly and as if suddenly seized by compassion, she said, "But you won't go without a special treat. I will make it myself with my own two hands, just like your mother!"

# *Little Red Riding Hood*

"All right, children, have a seat. Today is a big day! If you want, you can say a prayer—I've already prayed, as God knows, if he hasn't already forgotten."

I watched my father anxiously as he uttered these words with the air of someone who has an astonishing announcement to make but delays it so that he can keep his audience in suspense a little longer.

"I have a surprise for you," he went on in a delicate voice, full of emotion, keeping his eyes on our mother, who wouldn't remain seated at the kitchen table.

"Deborah, do you want to be part of today's joy?" he asked. "Even if you're not going to believe what I'm about to tell you, sit beside me. Your presence is essential."

Our mother had removed her shoes from the stove where she'd placed them to dry; they were old and as stiff as wood, emitting an awful stench that rose in little wafts up to the low ceiling. Mama moved about wearily, murmuring words of reproach directed at our father that we didn't need to catch to understand their meaning.

"Come here, Mama," we said in unison. "Don't make us wait or we'll all die of curiosity."

"Better that way," she said. "Maybe he'll tell you he's seen the ocean or found a gold mine!"



Our father's eyes filled up with tears and his lower lip began trembling slightly.

"Let Mama grumble. You can tell us!" we begged but he got up and left the house, slamming the door.

We remained seated, casting furtive glances at Mama, who was using a wooden knife to scrape mud from the heel of my little brother's shoe.

"I wonder what Papa was going to say," I ventured timidly.

Without pausing her work, Mama took aim at me in place of everyone else. "Here's something else I have to do! Because you're sitting and waiting for manna to fall into your mouths from heaven. If I don't go around asking for lard that's normally thrown away and I don't make soap out of it to sell, I'd like to see what you'd be eating with your father's big talk!"

"You never let him talk, Mama. Maybe one time he'll tell the truth. He'd groomed his beard before coming to the table, and today's not Friday, so he doesn't have to go to temple. I'm sure he was going to announce something big!"

"You have your father's imagination. Luckily, you're a girl, and in time you'll find a dope to bewitch outside of this house, leaving me a boy who has my character and sees the reality of everyday life. I'll find him a girl with a dowry."

"Where will Papa be?" I instinctively said to myself, but not so quiet that Mama couldn't hear it.

"Where do you think he will be? Where he always is, with goyim filling his belly with bacon and other filth. Then he sulks at home, saying he's not hungry. I've never seen such a heathen Jew."



"You're too harsh, Mama," I shouted. "You never let anyone in this house speak. I . . . I just want to die!"

"That's just theater, but without the lights or the applause," said Mama, as I ran away in tears.

When I returned, it was already nighttime, and I climbed into bed without saying a word. My mother's voice reached me from the other side of the curtain, where the big bed was. "Did you eat out with your father?"

"I didn't eat and I'm not hungry."

"All right, my dear. When you're hungry, you'll eat. On the bedside table there's coffee with just a little milk because they won't give us any more credit. And with saccharine because we're out of sugar and I'm waiting for your father to buy more."

"Go away!" I managed to say between sobs, while the idea that I'd offended my mother filled me with sorrow and shame.

But she said sweetly, "What is it, Aniko? Are you hungry?"

A second later, she was sitting on my bed in her night shirt, rubbing my head and saying in a low voice, "Wait, I put aside some sugar, in case someone got sick. I hid it. I'll heat up your coffee. Why are you crying? Is it something serious?"

"I only want coffee," I said, sniffling. "Put the sugar aside for Papa, for his bread."

"Are you afraid he won't be back?" my mother went on. "He'll be back, he'll be back. False money is never lost. Can't you see I'm standing here blowing on this damn stove? It's to keep his dinner warm. Your shoes are already nice and dry and clean for school tomorrow. So go to sleep now, my dear. Goodnight."



"Wait, Mama. Give me a kiss. And a hug. Two hugs."

While she was leaning over to kiss me, she murmured in a low voice, "How many things do you need? Do you know you're not a baby anymore? You're almost fifteen! Who can give you everything you need? How will you carry on when I'm gone?"

"Mama, you'll live forever because I love you too much," I shouted, still teary.

"You read too much poetry instead of praying," she said. "Try reciting with me now: 'Holy is the name of Adonai. . . .' "

The next morning, my first question was, "Where's Papa?"

"He went out," my mother said. "He'll be back for lunch."

"And did he tell you?"

"What? Don't be thinking I still remember. Go now and get ready, you have school."

"What am I supposed to do? I have to bring wood. The teacher asks me every morning and I don't know what to say because I'm ashamed to tell her we don't even have enough for our own house. Just give me four logs, Mama."

"Just what we needed with how much it costs!" she shouted. "Why doesn't the town or the government or someone, who knows, give it to her? Tell her your mother won't give it to you and leave it at that. What with the taxes still needing to be paid . . ."

At school, everyone brought their own wood and I made my excuses to the teacher, who gave only this comment: "Jews are stingy, naturally. Don't you like being warm? It's a shame I can't deprive only you three Jews of heat."



I was the first one to run out of school, and at home I found Papa surrounded by my younger siblings, who pestered him with questions that he deflected by saying, "Wait a second until we have everyone at the table. Oh, here you are Aniko. Deborah, where are you? Can you hear me?"

But Mama shouted from the stove, "Did you go and pay off the milk, Alex? They keep watering it down every day and I can't even argue, I have to just give thanks because we've owed for thirty-one days today. Look at it! It's now really water mixed with some milk, wouldn't you say?"

She shoved a pot half-filled with a bluish liquid under his nose.

"Exactly. What I wanted to say," my father babbled, "it seems that . . ."

"That what?" Mama shrieked. "Did you pay? Or are you going to pay tomorrow? It's always tomorrow, but which day is tomorrow?"

With his head hovering over the plate, he quickly gobbled up dumplings as he attempted to signal with his fork that he wanted to talk.

"Tomorrow!" my mother kept saying. "You'll talk tomorrow!"

"Children, I have a surprise."

He was now turning to us, since he saw my mother still wasn't listening to him.

But Mama said, "God only knows how many surprises there have been since we got married."

At that moment, I saw my father get to his feet quickly, overturning his seat, and then the glass door shattered into pieces as he howled from the yard, "I'll sell it myself!"

"Who would buy you?" came the reply from Mama, who had misheard and thought he had said, "I'll sell myself."

All of us children burst out laughing and we didn't stop even when my mother discovered the glass shards all over the floor. Her shouts then became high-pitched. "Why? Why does my religion forbid it? I would kill him! It's a miracle this house is still standing! Only by the power of the Divine Spirit."

I was already outside, away in the fields, and I could hear her shouts but her voice was muffled by the hum of dusk along the banks of the Tisza. Sitting on the grass, I listened to the frogs going "ribbit ribbit," and the voices of the birds in the woods that seemed like so many humans speaking different dialects without understanding each other and repeating the same things a thousand times, like Papa saying, "I mean that . . ." "ribbit ribbit . . ." And there he would stop, just like the frogs, the birds, and the woods.

I threw a few rocks in the river and watched them quickly vanish, swallowed up, like Papa with the dumplings. And I, too, would have liked to be swallowed up by the river, but my strength had given out and I lay down in the tall grass while my poor little mind repeated, "Mama doesn't change, just like Papa who's always making promises . . ."

"Aniko, Aniko! Where are you, my child?"

The clear voice of my mother coming from afar struck me like a bucket of icy water. I jumped to my feet and raced home, the voice growing louder.

"Aniko, come here! Papa has spoken! He's told us. He bought a cow that can give eight liters of milk."

In a burst, I sped past my mother who was crying with joy, and made my way into the yard. Not seeing my father, I hugged the cow, tearfully hanging on its neck. My father arrived with a woman while I was still clinging to the cow, repeating, "Little red riding hood, little red riding hood."

Mama, however, couldn't manage to say anything. It was our father's big moment and, turning to the woman, he said, "Come now, show them what it can do."

With a gentlemanly gesture, he made room for the woman, who sat down and began milking the cow to show my mother. Milk gushed into the bucket, as light and lively as our hearts.

My mother grew suspicious. "Alex, how did you come by a cow like this? Where is it from? Is there any possible way you were dishonest?"

The woman who was milking the cow kept an ear out but was disappointed because Papa began speaking in Yiddish. I was forced to go to great lengths to understand each word as my mother's face drained of all color and she repeated, "Oh Lord, oh Lord."

I was so excited that I let go of the cow and latched onto the leg of my father's pants so I wouldn't miss any part of the amazing story: A rich farmer had gotten a fifteen-year-old Jewish girl pregnant. It happened in the stables where there were some newborn lambs that the girl often visited. The farmer knew my father, told him everything, and justified it all by saying he'd heard from an acquaintance who lived in the city that Jewish women were warm and melancholy and worth more than their own women. When he spotted her there alone with her strange and beautiful eyes, he felt such desire, adding, "It didn't take much to lay her down."

"Never touched a Jewish woman before, and you being Jewish, you can understand," he said, looking my father in the eye. "But if word ever got back to my wife, it would be enough for her to lodge two bullets in my skull. You have to find a husband for this girl and then you can pick out my finest cow."

"And there she is," my father said, pointing to the cow, which was looking toward us in wonderment.

My mother's strength had given out. "You're a beast. You're worse than the godless."

“That’s enough now!” our father replied. “What if I hadn’t done it? Think of the sorrow for the girl’s parents. Consider her shame! Or the farmer who’d have been shot to death? Think of the innocent child yet to be born! How can you let so many people be ruined? Deborah, you never see beyond the prayer book. For once, lift your eyes and see the world for what it is! Don’t interrupt me—I beg you. This time, I’m doing the talking. I prevented one man’s death, I arranged a husband for this poor girl, a father for the baby . . . I saved two families from mourning and despair—you don’t think I even deserve a cow for my labors? You really don’t think so? Look in the bucket—it’s already full of life! Pure like my conscience. And how many more buckets will be filled yet.”



“You there! The one listening, spellbound,” my mother said, drying her eyes. “Go get another basin. Make yourself useful to your parents, and to other people, as your father has done!”

When I came back, they were embracing. My father was done talking and my mother was saying, “For now, we’ll go on like this, and the Almighty will be the judge.”

That didn’t seem real to my father.

“We can wait and see,” he said, “but we’re better off with the cow than without it, right, children?”

There was a lump in my throat. “First, I have to take a dip in the milk. There’s no water here, Mama. It’s real milk, and this time, I’m jumping in! I’m jumping in!”

# *Mr. Goldberg*

I RAN INTO FRIDA on the boulevard and I was so overjoyed at stumbling upon a familiar face that I circled her like a dog reuniting with his owner after a long time—but she didn't seem as happy to see me, which dampened my enthusiasm a little.

"When did you arrive?" she asked me.

"Four months after you," I replied, "exactly eight months ago."

Then I added jokingly, "You're already a *sabra*." I knew only native-born Israelis had the right to call themselves after the sweet, thorny prickly pear. "I bet you speak Hebrew and you've even found a job."

"I work as a waitress for a *yeke* at a restaurant in Mount Carmel."

"What's a *yeke?*" I asked Frida, laughing.

"You don't know they call German Jews *yekes* here?"

"So, you're not with your husband's friends?"

I'd met her in Germany when she was married to a Polish man.

"We divorced recently," Frida said, almost to herself. "It wasn't worth going on so now I work only for myself. Working as a waitress, you earn decent money. At my place, I have officials from the United Nations who leave good tips. Important people, but very demanding: one complaint and the *yeke* will fire you."

"The Germans are exacting even here," I replied bitterly.

We were walking up and down the main street in Haifa and it seemed like Frida hadn't caught my comment.

"What do you expect?" she said. "This is a tough time. We're only a few months into establishing this country, and peace and well-being are still far off. You can't get everything you want and right away. As soon as I arrived, I also wanted everything and I wanted it right away, as if the country owed me something—all of us who came from Europe with our luggage full of horrors. Now, after a year of living here, I am ashamed of my demands. I realize now that we owe something to the country."

"Are you done preaching?" Disappointed, I was nearly shouting.

Frida looked at me, and for the first time, she seemed to notice me.

"What's wrong?" she said sweetly. "Do you need something?"

I'd been pounding the pavement for three weeks looking for work, any kind of work, just to survive while beating back my pessimism, asking myself what I knew how to do and what I wanted to do, if I had a skill. And I kept replying that no, I didn't have a skill, but I'd do anything a woman could do.

Now Frida began quizzing me. "What languages do you speak?"

"A bit of all of them, if necessary. I get by."



"There's one thing you have to know: here Poles help Poles, Germans help Germans, Russians help Russians. And we Hungarians are last on the list for favors because we haven't managed to land anyone in key positions in the government and we don't have any influence in this country."

Whenever Frida spoke about the nation, her tone grew stronger, like a speaker who wants to convince the rebels, convert them to the good fight. But that morning my empty stomach rejected her sermons.

"Exactly how did you find a job?" I asked her angrily.

"Are you part of the *Histradut?*" Since I wasn't replying, she added, "You should enroll—it's more than a union. It's our alliance, it takes care of us from birth to death. They're the ones who helped me; I knew a boss there, a good friend. It's a shame he got transferred to Jerusalem."

She looked at me and smiled for the first time. Then she placed a hand on my shoulders and said, "With shoulders like these, why don't you work as a dockworker at the port?"

"I don't think it's that easy," I retorted. "They're

all Turks and Druse, or from Salonika, with a few Polish bosses."

"So join the army! You'll eat and sleep for free and you'll learn a profession. And you can move ahead."

I looked at her bitterly. "I've had enough of all the camps and all the uniforms in the world!"

"Oh right, you're not old enough," she said, paying me no mind. "Listen, when you're looking for a job, don't say you're not eighteen yet. When they ask you what you know how to do, say everything. If they ask what language you speak, say you speak all of them, and that you have experience in that type of job. If then they want some information, have them call my hotel, and I'll see to it that the boss talks you up as one of my relatives. And if you're hungry, stop by Café Carmelo where I can give you something for free whenever. You got it?"

She gave me other advice before we said goodbye, then we separated and she wouldn't hear of me thanking her. A light autumn mist was falling gently on the slick asphalt where many feet in sandals or clogs like mine traveled, but also many trucks and occasionally a car.

The air was still warm from that day's sirocco; I happily gave into getting soaked and I breathed in the pleasant scent of rain mixed with desert sand. A stronger aroma wafted out of kitchens in the neighborhood, one of aromatic spices and fried foods that gusts of wind slapped across our faces around every corner, every alley, every door. I lingered in front of a restaurant, watching the coming and going of waiters who waltzed by behind the glass with rows of plates balanced up to their elbows.

"They're all eating," I thought. "Those piggies!"

Hunger was harder to bear when you were alone rather than in a group. I'd experienced both kinds, but the first is far worse.



Inside there was a cacophony of orders and complaints, along with some shouting that even I could hear. "Bread, Zahava! Fish, Zahava! Oh, Zahava," they called out to the waitress, sometimes summoning her kindly and sometimes scolding her harshly. Shrugging, Zahava responded with a slight grin that showed a set of small teeth behind thin lips colored with a heavy lipstick the shade of ox blood. She raced from the tables to the cash register where she entered every order; she, too, must have had hungry countrymen who ate for free, but it couldn't have been easy to fool the owner who sat behind the counter, watching her every move. If she got up to answer the phone, a man—her husband?—took her spot. The waitress had dark skin, like the owners: almost certainly they were from Yemen. The owner yelled something toward the interior of the restaurant, where the kitchen likely was, and the waitress ran back and forth, smirking and scratching her head, then she removed a shoe while leaning on an empty table. Her swollen feet must have hurt, as she vigorously massaged them. People kept coming and going, even bumping into each other. I wished they'd ask me something, but what would I have said? That I was hungry? They wouldn't have believed me; another time, I said as much and they laughed in my face. *It's not possible that a pretty young girl is hungry.* I wanted to say hunger isn't partial to the ugly or the old neither does it ask one's age. Without realizing it, I pushed open the door of the restaurant, inside they were arguing with the waitress in Arabic and French. The Americans shouted the most, a real racket.

It appeared Zahava didn't understand all that well, but she kept saying, "Yes, yes, sir," with the same ever-ready smile, as if it were plastered between her tongue and her white teeth. The Americans were having a ball; they must have been mechanics or boilermen from a mercantile ship that had just arrived. You could see they were new here because they didn't try to get away with anything with the waitress. I spoke English well but standing in front of the counter, I was seized by that panicky shyness of mine, which I detected when I needed more confidence and strength. It was as if I was lost, and I stood there watching the slender, agile waitress who almost didn't appear to speak any language but who filled the small leather bag tied to her belt with bills and coins from every country with the confidence of a seasoned cashier. While she moved from table to table, I could hear the jingle of the coins banging against her belly like an Arabian dancer.

"Zahava!"

The husky but sharp voice made me turn around; it was the owner.

"Can't you see the young lady is waiting? Seat her."

The waitress didn't seem to hear her but automatically repeated, "Yes, ma'am. I'm coming right away, sir. It's ready."

"Oh Lord," I thought, "what will I say to her? And if they hire me, how will I walk back and forth on my flat feet? Here, you need healthy feet. And what language will I use with the waitress?"



Zahava pointed to a seat, really just an empty spot at a table where three people were eating. The three men gestured for me to sit down and I tried to explain to the waitress that I wasn't actually there to have a seat at a table.

Then the strict voice from before could be heard. "What does the young lady want?"

Without turning around, the waitress shrugged and continued to wait on tables, paying no attention to me.

"I'm looking for a job," I said to the woman in broken Hebrew.

Smiling, she got up and gave her spot to the other owner who immediately came over to the counter without ceasing to watch me slyly—two small, pale eyes that seemed buried in his round, olive-colored face.

The woman was fat, with endless gold bands on her bare arms, and her wrinkled skin reminded me of coarse, pilled fabric. Her clothes were stained with grease across her abundant, unrestrained bust, the immensity of which was daunting. My gaze shifted to the other owner, of whom all I could see was his upper body, clothed in a nylon shirt that was stuck to his gray chest hair. I knew right away I wouldn't be able to pull it off. All three of us looked at each other for a moment and then the woman asked where I was from.

"I'm Hungarian," I said.

"Oh!" they both said cheerfully. "You say, '*Igen migen hap die fligen.*' "

It was a nonsense phrase, half Yiddish and half Hungarian, a slight about us Hungarian Jews and our impossible language. They were laughing and I burst out laughing, too, over their awful pronunciation, not even stopping when they asked me about my work.

The two of them exchanged a knowing look and then the woman returned to the counter with a sarcastic smile on her face. She was now clearly feigning her sympathy, she must have thought I was a stupid fool, her opinion was already formed. The other owner moved closer to say they didn't need another waitress while he looked down my shirt and put his sweaty hand around my shoulders, unsure whether he should accompany me to the door.

The woman got up, but only so she could put herself between us. That was when I realized they were husband and wife.

"Go back to your spot, Rachel," the man said to his wife. The woman didn't move an inch but instead took hold of his hand and forced him to let go of my bare shoulder.

"Rachel," he repeated in a louder voice, "I told you to go back to your post."

The waitress quit making her rounds and watched us, with obvious pleasure. The flaming eyes of the woman owner bore down on me and, gathering myself up, I went out the door while the man murmured that I could come back when I wanted—that I had to come back.



It wasn't raining outside and it seemed like a lot of time had gone by since I'd entered the restaurant to ask for work; one world inside there and a different world out here where the wind had quieted down to a light breeze that dried the rain from before off the roofs and the streets. The air tickled my face with an affectionate, familiar hand. I felt love for my country, which was so clean, with young trees lining the streets of the German quarter and flowers that had rebounded with the recent rain. By the side of the road where I was walking, two rows of solid stone homes inspired confidence: people exited the buses and hurried toward home, laborers returned from work tired, with leftovers from lunch wrapped in a nylon pouch tucked under their arms—the poorer ones with the remains of their snacks in a paper bag. I knew this because even my brother used to go to his shift with something I'd prepared for him, and he always brought back the rest, which he would need the next day. I was the only one who walked without any haste, without a destination, with no one waiting for me. But time was worthless now, because I had so much of it on my hands, whether I liked it or not. I said to myself, "With all this time before me, the minutes seem that much longer, given my hunger." To break up the wait, I asked a passerby if he could tell me the time.

"I'm busy," he replied. "I don't know if I'll make the last run heading out for Tira."

A lot of effort to not tell me the time. Perhaps it was six o'clock in the afternoon, when the last buses left the terminal before the Saturday holiday began.



Children's voices and laughter arose from the yard of one of the homes; two children with their damp hair freshly washed and combed were playing. The brass handle of the gate must have been newly polished, and it sparkled like the lamps at home that I had cleaned as a child every Friday afternoon while my mother heated on the stove large crocks of water, which she then poured into enamel basins and we seven children argued about who would be washed last. Once, I was like that, blonde and happy like the little girl with pale eyes who approached me, threatening me with a water gun.

"What's your name?" I asked, and as she replied she pulled the trigger, aiming at my eyes, which were already wet.

Since I didn't react, she burst into joyful laughter, shouting, "Fight back! Why don't you fight back?" She had fun watching me as I stood there with my face wet under fire from her gun, which no longer shot water even though she kept pressing the trigger with her tiny hands. The gun, now useless, was thrown to the ground and, speaking half in German, half in Hebrew, she summoned her brother for help.

The two of them stared at me, the little boy calling to his mother in a desperate voice, the little girl letting out shrieks that reminded me of the sound of the pigs when, before Christmas, the farmers in my village would slip their knives under their jaws again and again until they'd cut their throats. Afterwards, the stench of roasted flesh pervaded the village and we children would run in the blistering cold to the yard where a wood fire was burning with a single spit for the pigs, which slowly browned. Women would rush about with pots full of water, or busy themselves preparing spices to season tripe or for filling sausage casing with salami. We'd stand on a single foot and the child who could hold out the longest won the grilled pig's tail. I played along for fun, not to win anything—because Jews cannot touch pork—until my mother called me back home and I would reply in the high-pitched voice I had back then, "Coming, Mama!" Inside the house, Mama would say, "Dinner will be ready soon. Be quick, your father is about to return from the synagogue. Come inside now!"



All mothers are that way on Friday evenings when they say, "Come inside, don't get dirty, your father is coming and soon we'll eat." I knew every syllable of those words, and I mimicked my mother when she would say, "We're going to eat soon, come inside children. Don't make a mess."

I looked at my soaked blouse; the water had combined with a day's worth of dirt to create long brown streaks. I had walked so long and my stomach was empty! With Saturday approaching, even the streets were empty. I headed for home but I couldn't stretch out on my bed until I'd done something to quiet my hunger a bit. I came across a store that was still open and without a moment's thought, I went inside to buy some bread.

"I'd like two loaves like that one, the braided kind," I said.

"We're closing now and those have already been sold," a woman said.

"May I have just one—dark or black? One of any kind, I have no bread in the house for tomorrow."

"It's all sold," the woman said. "But you can try farther along at the Hungarian pharmacist's shop. You're also Hungarian, right?"

"Yes, but I'd take any kind of bread."

While I was talking, the woman lowered the shop's shutters, leaving me alone on the street while she remained inside the darkened grocery store.

I said nothing more, not even the special Saturday greeting that I liked so much, trying instead to say it to myself: "Shabbat Shalom." But I felt my throat close up, threatening to suffocate me. I bumped into an old man with a beard who was pushing a four-wheeled cart containing drinks and sweets.

"Can't you see?" he said in Yiddish.

"Would you give me some biscuits, please?" I asked him.

"I can't, the Sabbath has already begun and I can't touch money. I'm late, I didn't even make it to the synagogue. What would people say if they saw me working?"

He was pushing his cart and I ran behind him, doggedly asking for the biscuits, at least one packet.

"Please be kind," I begged. "I know you can no longer handle money but I'll pay you on Sunday when you come through this area again. I see you pass every day, I know you . . ."

He paused for a moment and pulled out a large box of chocolate wafer packets.



"Could I have two?" I hastened to ask. "It's the same thing."

"Hmph," he grumbled crossly, then he pointed at the box. "Drop the money in here so that I don't have to touch it."

"I don't have any money," I said quietly.

"What?!" the old man shouted. "Are you mocking me?"

He made as if to take back the two packets of cookies. I would never have given them back to him, I was squeezing them tightly in my hands like a child from whom one wants to take away a favorite toy. I felt my blood rise to my cheeks while my heart was beating hard.

"I'll pay for them," I babbled. "They cost so little. I swear that I'll have some money to pay you."

The old man with the beard stared at me with two penetrating eyes that definitely knew how to read someone's mind because he opened the big box again, took out two more packets and handed them to me. Then he filled a glass with fizzy water.

"Drink this and follow me home. Where six of us eat, seven can eat. He grunted the name of the street and the house number, convinced I would follow him as he quickly moved along with his cart. I was hurrying, too, but toward my room, where I threw myself on the bed to wolf down the four packets of cookies. Once I'd quieted some of my hunger, I was able to evaluate the situation. Undressing, I thought perhaps I'd make a mistake not following the old man. I remembered the name of the road he'd said—Giaffa Street—but as for the number, I'd find it, there couldn't be that many old men with a cart as well as a beard in that street. They would give me a nice meat or fish soup, I didn't care which, with a big piece of slow-cooked meat, or who knows what other things the wife would have prepared for dinner? My father always used to eat two plates, plus our leftovers, which we raced to scrape onto his plate, saying mirthfully, "Here, eat this! You're a bottomless pit!" How happy we were on Friday nights, especially when we began with a fish course because inevitably meat followed. "A dinner fit for a king," my mother would say. "You can all thank heaven and lick all ten of your fingers."

Falling asleep, I dreamt of my father who looked like the man with the beard. He was old in my dream, and I resisted because I knew very well I was dreaming, having him resemble the old man in the street who had given me the biscuits. Then I heard my name called: "Barbara, aren't you going to pray with us? Repeat after me: God, please bless our Saturday bread and may your name be praised for all of eternity. Amen." In that moment, I could clearly see my father, it was him, I strained to open my eyes so I could see him better—but opening them fully, I woke up. Groggy from sleep, I tried to remember every detail of the dream but came up short because I was hungry again. I got up to get something to drink, then I went back to lying on the bed, forcing myself to dream of an entire roast goose for me, and repeating the words my mother would say to us children in the lean days, after we'd had a dinner of only tea and bread, "The hungry pig dreams of acorns."

Waking the next day, I felt as though I'd been transformed into a paragon of will and faith. I wanted to find a job and one job only: a waitress in a restaurant, so as to be constantly near dishes, hot food, and money. As I looked at myself in the mirror (one's appearance is important when looking for work), I saw my little room reflected back: a narrow, white bed that was the kind used by elderly people and old folks' homes, and for a closet, an iron bar where two blouses hung. No table, no curtains. Before I left, I arranged an old military blanket on the uneven tile floor.

I'd decided to begin my search methodically, neighborhood by neighborhood, street by street. I didn't expect there to be so many restaurants by the port. In the windows, there were generous displays of all the Saturday delicacies, and the waiters watched me quickly come and go after I'd exchanged a few words with the owner. The response was always the same: "We don't need anyone." But I wasn't any more nervous than the day before; I took the rejections with a smile and tried two doors down. By about noon, I'd already finished up with the restaurants by the port;

only the grand restaurants along the waterfront were left. I wasn't tired and I wasn't hungry; in my head, I'd already furnished my room with my first paycheck as a waitress. I'd chosen the fabric for the curtains and thrown out the military blanket for a beautiful, authentic rug from Yemen. I was debating between a chest and a wardrobe with a mirror, and I didn't know whether there would be enough money for all that furniture and a green blouse with short sleeves that I'd admired in a store in Nordau Street.

The restaurant had a wide terrace, which was deserted at that hour, while the inside was jammed with people of every nationality. I struggled to find my way because there were two cash registers and both were vacant. Walking by me was a pale, overwrought waiter with circles under his eyes who was so thin that I began entertaining sunny notions about his replacement.

"Where is the owner?" I asked.

"Why are you asking?" he said.

"I'd like to speak with him," I said calmly, determined not to be overcome by a bossy manner that was at odds with the hang-dog smile he rolled out for the occasion. But a voice like that of a rooster rather than a man, a high voice, coming from the back of the room, made him jump.

"What does the girl want, Adolf?" the voice asked.

"I think she's looking for a job," Adolf said turning to a table where four men were sipping their coffee. I didn't know who the voice could possibly belong to, since the four men were all massive in size, until the largest of the four got up and came toward me. Instead of saying hello, he asked my name.

"Barbara," I said.

"Very well," he replied. "My name is Mr. Goldberg and that's what you are to call me."

Then, sizing me up from my sandals to my bare shoulders, he said, "We might need an attractive girl like you. We're getting into summer and a dead man walking like Adolf isn't right for the terrace."



He laughed with his high, squeaky voice. "Let's sit at this table, which is reserved for me," he said, then shouting toward the kitchen, added, "Abdullah! Two Turkish coffees!"

All of my confidence disappeared and I observed him by casting furtive glances at his body, while carefully avoiding his eyes. He had short legs that dangled from his seat and were capped by two small, ladylike feet shod in pointed, shiny leather shoes. His arms were even shorter, and his well-groomed hands had unusually long nails for a man. His generous belly reminded me of my sister when she was expecting a baby and given her upside-down pear shape, everyone said it would be a boy, and then instead it was a girl. The only pleasant thing about him was the lemony scent of cologne that emanated from his obese body.

As soon as he realized I was studying him, his small, red-rimmed eyes opened wide and he made a stunned, sorrowful face, like that of a mouse caught in a trap. Then he asked me in an indifferent tone, "Do you find me ridiculous?"

"No, no Mr. Goldberg," I said fearfully.

"Well then don't give me such an idiotic look. So, what can you do beyond looking at me that way?"

"I can do everything," I said with an assured voice that surprised even me.

"Good," he said. "I like decisive people. We'll get along just fine because you don't know how to do a darn thing but you've just told me you can do it all as if on a dare. Let's have a coffee, though, and then we'll talk about work."



Talking to himself, he kept saying, "Yes, yes, I like you. I like women who lie because you won't make anything in this business if you tell the truth—no one will believe you. But raise your head and look me in the eye when I speak to you," he added in a commanding voice. "Always look people in the face, smile, be cheerful. If you learn these three rules, you will do a good job serving and the world will serve you!"

He smiled, pleased with himself. "I have another rule. I explain everything right away and once. If you work here, you'll make a note of that."

"Yes, sir! I want to work," I said quickly.

"Don't call me sir and don't interrupt me when I'm talking," he said, with a voice that left me defenseless. "Learn to listen."

Reddening, I said to myself, "I'm going to be quiet now. I'll sew my mouth shut. I won't say anything more except, 'Yes, Mr. Goldberg.'"

I began to tremble, which was difficult to conceal.

"When you speak," he went on with his lecture, "look happy. The world has had enough of seeing gloomy faces like yours. Happiness is hard to come by and everyone is looking for it. If you're asked how you are, don't say good or bad. Say, 'I'm doing OK.' That's another rule of mine because if you say you're doing 'very well,' either they don't believe you or they're jealous. If you say, 'I'm down in the dumps,' you'll make them happy and that's not OK either. Stick to the middle and you'll never get it wrong. You see the table Adolf is serving. What type of people are sitting there, in your opinion?"



I looked at the waiter who was serving a ham omelet to a table of two elegant, made-up women who were happily chatting away.

"I don't know," I said in a whisper, "they could be nobility, women who are fabulously wealthy."

"They're streetwalkers," Mr. Goldberg said. "You fool! You don't know how to recognize people by their appearance. If you want to be a waitress, you have to size people up at first glance, read what's in their pockets as well as their hearts, calculate their worth, and then offer them something to eat and drink, you got it? There are customers who want the set price meal and those who want the menu, a word used by the fancier people who also ask to see the wine list. The diners club card is good only for the regulars and the Israeli citizens, not the foreign crews and mission delegations. You have to know how to recommend the more expensive items, the refrigerated dishes, the cold cuts and the chops. Pay attention: those eating the once-a-week meat ration have to give you the coupon book so you tear off a meat coupon. For them, the price is capped, but without the coupon book meat costs much more and can't be served to everyone. You have to judge the customer because it may be someone from the fiscal office and then we're in trouble if the person isn't a friend. The price also changes depending on the customer."

Then smiling, he added, "The noble ladies can have anything they want but the price is the same for all of them otherwise they will shout and scratch your eyes out if they're having a bad day. Policemen, healthcare workers, night watchmen, bankers and tax office employees—I know them all and I'll take care of them."



My head hurt from the lesson, which was so unfamiliar and full of new things.

"And don't give me that stupid look. I know it's not easy, they come especially from the port, people who work on the ships, who pay using dollars, crowns, pounds, lira, dracmas, florins, rubles, all of which you have to learn to recognize, divide, add and subtract mentally before you bring the bill to the counter. One can earn well with ships at the port. You'll also earn as much as you want if you can remember that legally only the official prices are valid. We don't serve drunks, I have my men who see to that."

He winked in a way that I didn't understand.

"The sailors will ask you out on dates; you smile and say yes to everyone and you don't go out with anyone. I'll keep an eye on you as far as that's concerned. That's why I am here. You'll earn honestly enough to live. Do you have a man? Are you married?"

"It's just me," I replied.

"It's better that way," he said. "I still need to tell you that as part of your pay you get ten percent of what you ring up each day in addition to tips. I won't say anything about honesty because I'll bring charges the first time I notice anything missing. Do we understand each other? Or aren't you listening? What are you looking at?"

"Is everything in the refrigerator on offer?" I asked meekly.

"Just about," Mr. Goldberg said. "The smoked tongue is for me, the goose pate is for the shipowner Lebovitsch and the banker Halevy, who will be coming later. The caviar I'm leaving for the Russians."

My head swung from the refrigerator to the counters in the kitchen which I glimpsed through the swinging door and my deepest wish in that moment was to open the refrigerator door, throw myself on the platters and eat and eat and eat until I died.

"I wish I was a dog on a chain," I thought to myself. "I'd break the chain and I'd pounce on the kitchen counters. But how can I tell this portly man that I'm hungry and how do I turn into a dog? When I was a little girl, I believed in magic wands. One flick and I'd have a table set for me only, with Mr. Goldberg himself serving me sterling silver plates of goose pate and smoked tongue with spicy peppers like my grandfather used to eat come winter."

In my confusion, I could hear his voice talking about good clients and bad clients but I was swimming in a pool of fabulous sauces and marzipan cream,

I was eating and drinking, even choosing the dishes I liked best.

"What's wrong? Are you crying?" the same squeaky voice rattled me, snapping me back to reality. "I hate tears, and don't thank me—I haven't hired you yet. You'll have to work for it if you want to stay on. You need me just like I need you, and we're equals. You'll start tomorrow, today is Saturday, enjoy the day off, you won't get many after that."

Then he added, "You know what? Let's have a little tryout. Go over to my wife and ask for my usual lunch. Scram!"

I hadn't moved, and this bothered him.

"You have to get moving!" he shouted. "To get ahead in life, use your elbows. How do you think I got where I am? What, are you still crying?"

I couldn't hold back the tears anymore. I saw a woman approach and I could see her pale, muscular legs, with bulging veins and a pair of wide, thick-soled shoes. Slowly, I raised my head. A tall, formidable woman stood before me, and she watched me with two eyes awash with profound sadness. She made brisk, uptight movements. Her mouth, framed by two bitter folds furrowing into her face, mustn't have known how to smile.

"You! The one doing all the preaching! How do you know how someone feels and what someone wants if you don't even know your wife who you've been living with for thirty years? What do you know about feelings and tears? What are you talking about if you're not even able to see this girl is hungry?"

Mr. Goldberg was speechless but only for a moment because he immediately recovered.

"You're a good woman," he said, turning to his wife. "It's too bad we've never understood each other."

Turning toward me, he shouted cheerfully, "You idiot! You couldn't have said you were hungry?"

"You didn't notice it!" his wife said icily. Then she took my hand. "Come! I'll have Adolf serve you. Order whatever you want."

She pushed me toward a table with a white tablecloth just for me, where Adolf was arranging three or four plates full of antipastos and cold cuts. I quietly fell upon the various dishes.

Adolf stood a short distance away, in a white jacket, watching me. "You eat more than Mr. Goldberg. It takes a lot to outdo him. He needs a waiter all for himself. We don't work for free here."

"But you always get to eat here?" I asked.

Adolf looked at me curiously and didn't respond.

I went on. "And you're paid, too?"

"If you know what you're doing. And if you get on his good side," he said, gesturing toward the massive size of Mr. Goldberg with an empty plate I'd handed him.

"Bring me another beer, Adolf, and more bread. A lot more bread. I feel like a queen today, so serve me. Tomorrow I'll begin serving, too."

I was already seeing things more clearly, and I was ready to swear by the goodness of my fellow man and cry over the world's generosity.

Stunned, Adolf said, "You're crying again?"

"You have to give vent even to your happiness," I said. "Bring me more white bread. Today is Saturday and I'm celebrating. My new life starts tomorrow, the future is bright, and it's like I love the whole world."

"Me, too?" Adolf joked.

"I don't like your name," I said, "but it's not your fault."

Adolf walked away, frowning, and I had to run after him to say I was joking and that we'd be good friends.

"Tomorrow we'll work together," I said, "and everything will be so easy! Wherever you have full plates, there must be leftovers."

I looked around and I didn't see a single sad face in the packed dining room.

"See you tomorrow!" I bellowed, smiling at everyone.

"*Shalom*," Mr. Goldberg said. "Six o'clock sharp."

"Without a doubt, Mr. Goldberg," I kept shouting as I left the restaurant. "Yes, Mr. Goldberg! Yes, sir."

# *Matzoh Bread*

PASSOVER FOR US JEWS always falls in April, and finding myself just then in Greece, I had a great desire to be with family, any family, so I could revisit and remember a bit of my childhood. I knew that if I went to synagogue, I would be invited to a home, as foreign Jews always are, because this is a day you cannot be alone—everyone must be with a family, no matter which one.

I had a few hours to decide if I should go or not. I had just arrived from Israel in a country where I didn't know anyone and where no one understood Hungarian, my language, much less Hebrew or Yiddish; would they understand my joys and my sorrows? I walked through the streets, telling myself, "The next person I see who looks even slightly familiar I will stop with some excuse, perhaps only to exchange a few words. But in which language? And can you really tell someone is Jewish by appearance, like the Germans claimed?"

I walked around for hours without mustering the courage to stop anyone. I went to the crowded cafes in town for a better chance of meeting someone. Athens was full of American men looking to win over the beautiful Helens, but they didn't seem prepared to wage war over one. They spent a few dollars, or a lot of drachmas, promising them America between whiskeys. I stopped for a pastry and a coffee, and I asked the boy working at the café the way to the synagogue. I wanted to see people that day, as many people as I could. I studied the faces of those rushing in and out of the synagogue, searching for someone with a friendly, less distracted gaze. I imagined that in their bags and packages there must be unleavened bread, wild herbs, a bottle of wine, and other things that were expressly enjoyed in the seven days of Passover. In the cheerful bustle around the synagogue, no one noticed me. But not even my thoughts were in Athens at that point.

What a joy Passover was for us as children, when we would step out onto our narrow muddy road in the afternoon, so careful in our new clothes, and before we turned the corner, we would look back at our mother, who stood there lifting her apron, white with flour, to dry her tears. It seemed as though centuries had passed since then, in the great darkness of annihilation, and not that a few years divided us from the past, from my school and my dear friends, one of whom was closer to me than a sister. Her name was Ilona, and it was for her that I stole a few pieces of matzoh from the kitchen while my mother had her back to me, busy at the oven. For us, it was a sacrifice, but I was so fond of Ilona and I wanted her to be fonder of me. That's why I tried to win her over with kindness.



"Guess what I brought for you, Ilona!" I said.

"I don't know," she replied. "Tell me."

"It's Jewish bread, as you would call it. It's good with coffee."

She turned from me, terrified. Cursing and shouting for me to leave, she said she would never eat any of that bread!

Once home, I tried to get my mother to explain Ilona's refusal, but she considered it a matter of little importance, saying only that there were more intelligent questions that I could ask, that she didn't have time to waste on silly disputes between girls, and she scolded me for the matzoh I'd taken, which I now held crumbled in my hand.

A few days went by, and I was no longer thinking about what happened when I saw Ilona appear at our door. Thrilled, I ran towards her, certain she was coming to apologize, but my friend stood before me without saying hello, pulled something out from under her arm, and angrily rubbed it on my lips and nose. It left a nauseating smell on me. When I was able to break free, I saw that it was a strip of pork fat, which was forbidden in our religion.

"Why don't you eat this? Go on—eat it!" she said, and then raced away, shouting insults against us Jews.

I stood there for a long time with the fatty taste on my mouth, searching for a response to such meanness.

"Mama," I said, "I'm begging you, tell me what unleavened bread is made of."

"You should know. I've already told you why we eat matzoh. You know what Passover means for us, right?" she said. "It's a bread made without yeast, only flour and water. That's it."

"And why do Christians refuse to eat it?" I persisted.

"Anyone can eat it if they want," she replied. "And now you know everything."

But I didn't know everything, and as soon as I saw Ilona again, I tried to talk to her, promising my set of shiny silver and gold foil paper that she had always liked. But this matter was so important that when I realized she couldn't be easily persuaded to talk, I promised her money. She'd never seen a pengő in her whole life, not even when she went for groceries, since farmers used what they grew to barter in shops and at the market.

The only hope I had of getting money was to watch my father as he slept; during the muggiest afternoons, he would go inside to sleep with his vest still on, and as he rolled over in bed, change would fall out of his pockets. I often gathered the change and brought it to my mother. That day, it took a while to convince my father to get some sleep, telling him he looked wearier than usual. Ilona had seemed willing to take the money I offered and I risked everything to have everything. After an hour, I'd collected a few coins, which I hid in my mouth. I ran out, headed for Ilona's house, not bothering to answer when my mother shouted after me, "Where are you going? And what do you have under your tongue?"

My friend was leaning against the hedge and pretended not to see me. Breathless but with a firm voice, I said to her, "Start talking—I have the money. Here's the foil paper. Take it. But the money I'll give you after you talk."



At the sight of the money, Ilona softened. She took my hand and led me away, behind the house.

"You see," she said, "the bread you Jews eat is made with the blood of Christians! Sometimes before Passover, a child disappears. . . . The people who make that bread kill him. . . ."

"That's a lie! None of that is true!" I shouted, before running home to relay the story.

My mother said she knew these nasty tales because one day a boy had disappeared and they had found him at a Jewish family's house. The legend had circulated in the village since then, with the locals recounting that the Jews wanted to kill the boy because it was Passover and they needed him to make their bread.

"Now do you see?" my mother said. "Do you understand the lies and the ignorance? And to help you understand even better, here's a smack because you stole money from your father, and another one because you paid attention to that garbage! If you need to know something, come to me."

Many years have passed since then—centuries, for

me—and my questions have piled up, even though my mother can no longer respond. I learned that unleavened bread is made of flour and water. And I also learned that they made soap from the flesh of millions of Jews in the camps, but I didn't have to steal any money from my father to discover it, and this time, no one said, "It's a myth."

"Why," I wanted to shout, "isn't it a myth like before? Why? Why isn't my father coming out of synagogue in his jacket, patched up for the holiday? Why can't my mother step out of the house anymore in her white dress, pure and spotless as she was?" But there wasn't anyone to hear me and the only warmth I felt came from the tears that ran down my cheeks to my lips.



I spent the day shuttling between the street and the hotel, as I waited for the service at the temple. Finally, night fell; as soon as it was dark, I was the first person to arrive at the synagogue and I waited for someone to let me in. I would have preferred to go inside alone, but a crowd soon formed, and I was dragged along without even a chance to choose my seat. The service bore no relation to my girlhood memories and I couldn't manage to connect to any of it. Just as when I had arrived, I felt myself dragged outside amid the private cars and taxi traffic. An old man was trying to manage the crowd by sorting everyone, putting them in groups, having them make introductions, and showing them to the cars. Mine was a cream-colored American car, and I found myself with other one-time invitees as the owner of the car drove home through the downtown streets and then past the Acropolis toward the sea.

When we pulled up to the villa, other guests were waiting. We all climbed up to the luxurious apartment, and I sat down at an enormous table with at least thirty people of different nationalities. Even the celebration at the house was different from the one my father gave. Huge silver platters full of bitter herbs and matzoh circulated constantly above my head. The table was festooned with elegant plates, crystal glasses, and cutlery in every size, the vast array embarrassing me. The many servers moved about the house, save one who was stationed by the telephone, which rang continuously. Every so often, she communicated a message to the lady of the house, a smiling, showy woman covered in jewels, who got up only for the most important calls, leaving in her wake a strong scent of perfume. Her husband was Russian, with a sturdy, smug face covered in freckles. He worked in import-export—successfully, no doubt. He seemed full of life, even though he was in up in years, and very witty, judging by the laughter that punctuated every joke he told; the women laughed the most.

He handed me a *coupe* of champagne, which gave me a chance to admire the huge gemstone on the pinky finger of his fleshy, white hand.

I thought of my parents, who didn't have fragrances or jewels; my father who would sit at the head of the table holding the Haggadah with his bony hands, his fingernails cleaned for the holiday, whose lean, sad face I glimpsed just before he bent his head in prayer. Every now and again he skipped a page, careful that my mother didn't notice, and doing so, he would wink at us children. I watched him, and when our eyes met, we laughed like two accomplices. Our kitchen table was small, its white damask tablecloth from my mother's trousseau was brought out only on important occasions. The candles, cut in half to save money, gave off a modest amount of light. My mother would pray with her hair covered by a white scarf that I bought her at the market. Once, while we were right in the middle of the Passover meal, my brother, Endre, and I burst out laughing; we began giggling at the most solemn moment for no reason at all. My father raised his head from the prayer book, got up from the table and asked us to come outside. Then with a wet rope, he whipped us on our legs and above, while we laughed and cried at the same time.



Now silver dishes danced before my eyes, course after course came out, but my plate always went away full. I could hear people talking and laughing all around me, and the telephone ringing in the distance. The owner of the house smiled at me every now and again, in an increasingly less formal way. The others paid no attention to me. Suddenly I got up, and asked the maid to find my coat under a pile of furs. I mumbled my thanks in English and paused in front of a little girl. She was the age I had been when I lost everyone and everything. I wished her much happiness. Out in the street, the cool air awoke me from my daydreams and the aroma emanating from the Greek restaurants made me hungry, but I had no regrets for the food on the silver platters.

When I arrived at the hotel, I raced up the five flights of stairs and threw myself on the bed, openly sobbing, alone with myself, and vowing that the next day I would have bread, a massive amount of bread, even if my religion forbade it, and I'd never ever again think about anything that reminded me of Passover.

# *Translator's Note*

WHEN I FIRST read the work of Edith Bruck, I was a young mother who had suddenly been made very aware of the perspectives of young children—most especially my son, Leo. He was about five years old when I read "Silvia," a wartime story that features an eleven-year-old German boy who rescues a Jewish stowaway in the woods near his house. I was struck by Bruck's decision to imagine a narrator who is the son of Nazis and to juxtapose him with a Jewish character. This choice of hers contributed to a sense that she was showing me aspects of the Holocaust I'd never before glimpsed in the work of male authors, and it drew me to her writing.

As I approached this work, I struggled with how to translate what can scarcely be imagined—especially by someone like me, born in the United States decades after World War II—and this was one of the questions

I posed when I had a short fellowship at the New York Public Library to conduct research for my translation. How to convey such a wrenching scene as Beni and Lenke being deported in the title story, "This Darkness Will Never End"?

Specific instances of vocabulary can provide a window into this dilemma. In the course of "Silvia," for example, Bruck uses various words connected to the verb "lamentare" no fewer than ten times, ranging from "lamento" to "lamentela" and "lamento collettivo." They are used in reference to passengers on a Nazi transport train and to the young stowaway who has miraculously escaped it. These words voice the horror of the Nazi regime that hovers over the story. They also likely voice something that Bruck herself experienced—the "lamenti" that she and her own family heard or expressed while being deported.

The verb "lamentare" is quite common in Italian conversation, and the form used most frequently expresses simple, garden-variety complaints. But here we have the noun form, which expresses something much deeper than a gripe.

During my New York Public Library fellowship, I set about doing comparative translational research. On a hunch that forms of "lamentare" might recur in survivor accounts, I spent time studying several works in Italian by other women writers who survived the Holocaust, including Liana Millu's *Il Fumo di Birkenau*. I searched Millu's text, along with Lynne Sharon Schwartz's English translation of it, and found that Millu also frequently used forms of "lamentare," which Schwartz translates variously as "moan," "groan," and "wail." The third option—wail—feels closest to the extreme emotion of the passengers who have been deported, and I have used it often in my translation.

There are words in addition to "lamentare" that recur, including, of course, the Italian word for darkness, which Bruck wields with such feeling. In Italian, it's the magnificent, vowel-heavy *buio*. In the mouth of Beni, in the collection's title story, it embodies all the injustice and all the uncertainty he is facing. The word dazzles me in Italian—its sound, the row of three vowels lined up in a way that so rarely occurs in English. But it's also a heavyweight when translated, albeit with an entirely different sound: darkness.

It's not surprising the word recurs in these stories. As I noted in the preface, the darkness will never end for Edith Bruck. But by peering into that darkness, she gives us the light of truth.

## *About the Author*

**Edith Bruck** is the author of more than twenty books of fiction, nonfiction, and poetry, and she has devoted her life to testifying about the Holocaust through her work, starting with *Who Loves You Like This* (1959, Italian edition; 2001, English edition, Paul Dry Books). Bruck is a transnational writer who was born in Hungary in 1931 but has been writing in Italian for more than fifty years. She has twice been a finalist for the Strega award, Italy's highest literary prize, including most recently for *Il pane perduto* in 2021 (*Lost Bread*, 2023, English edition, Paul Dry Books). Her book, *Lettera alla madre* (English title: *Letter to My Mother*, MLA Texts and Translations, 2006) won the Rapallo award in 1989. She also won the Viareggio prize for her novel, *Quante stelle c'è nel cielo*. Her books have been translated into many languages including English, French, German, Dutch, Polish, Hungarian, and Hebrew. Bruck has also translated the work of beloved Hungarian poets. Shc has spent decades speaking to Italian schoolchildren about the Holocaust. She lives in Rome.

## *About the Translator*

**Jeanne Bonner** is a writer, editor, and literary translator. Her essays and reporting have been published by *The New York Times*, *Brevity*, *The Boston Globe*, *American Scholar*, *Longreads*, *NPR*, and CNN. She was a 2022 NEA literature fellow in translation. She also won the 2018 PEN Grant for the English Translation of Italian. Her translations have appeared in *Asymptote Journal*, *Consequence*, *PEN America*, and the *Kenyon Review*. She lives in Connecticut where she works as an editor and writing instructor.